MCGINNIS WEREWOLVES

A HEROES RUN IN PACKS NOVEL

NEW YORK TIMES BESTSELLING AUTHOR

SHAWNTELLE MADISON

VALKYRIE
RISING
PRESS

McGinnis Werewolves

ebook ISBN: 978-1-7344510-6-1

Print ISBN: 979-8-6978705-7-0

Version 2.5

Edited by MK Books Editing, Edits720

For everyone who searched for hope against hope. You will find it someday.

[1]

For a werewolf hunter, being in the right place at the right time was crucial.

Unfortunately for Zach, he wasn't the hunter, but the hunted.

Zach surveyed the empty diner outside of Seattle. The hard guitar riffs from the rock classic, "Black Dog," from Led Zeppelin belted through the jukebox on the far side of the room. A few tables needed clearing from the last patrons, but otherwise he had the place to himself. He considered his piss-poor odds at escape. One entrance in the front. Another in the rear through the kitchen. Glass windows everywhere.

The bell attached to the door jingled.

Guess the diner wasn't empty anymore.

Five guys waltzed in wearing nondescript jeans and heavy coats, the scent of firearms and sweat heavy in their clothes. They sat in the booths on the other end of the room. The Red werewolf hunting clan had found him.

Anticipation seeped into him. Another fight was coming. If he closed his eyes, he could faintly hear their conversation over the music.

Werewolf hearing came in handy.

"You can't keep running from us, McGinnis," the clan sage, Old Bart, had told him. When Zach's old werewolf hunting team had cornered him in Missoula, Montana, he'd bitten off more than he could chew.

They'd nearly killed him, but he survived long enough for a werewolf's bite to save his life. Now that he played for team werewolf, he was still on the run while trying to figure out how to be a werewolf.

There was nothing like on-the-job training.

Another party entered the diner. Two men in black coats, stocky enough to be considered hired security, surveyed the room and ushered a woman to the west side of the diner. The beautiful Black woman smelled of money: lush floral perfume and the faint hint of expensive leather from a luxury vehicle. Expensive rings glinted off her fingers, and a long ivory dress peeked out from under her luxurious mink coat. Zach glanced at her, and when their gazes connected, the hairs on the back of his neck rose.

Very bad news, the wolf within warned him. *She isn't human.*

One waitress approached the party. Only the woman ordered a coffee. No cream. Five sugars.

From the other side of the room, one of the Red clan members shifted. Zach turned away from them. Far enough for the group to not see the Kimber Warrior handgun in his hand, but close enough for him to see them make their move.

And it would come. He had less than three minutes.

An olive-skinned woman from the kitchen walked up to the counter where he sat. "Want to order some food?"

He glanced up at her, and his breath caught.

"Zach?" The dark-haired woman's mouth parted slightly. "It is you, isn't it?"

How differently did he look compared to before he became a werewolf? The last time he'd taken in his face in the mirror, there'd been an edge to the glint in his hazel eyes. A harshness to the sharp angles in his face.

Damn it all to hell, he'd found her. *Lark.*

"Yeah." He bit back a sigh. Now wasn't the time for a reunion with the woman he'd left behind without a word less than a year ago.

He had his reasons for leaving, but now wasn't the time to discuss them with her.

"Wow…" Lark frowned, and her warm welcome vanished. "I prayed long and hard for months for a chance to cuss your ass out. Little did I know you'd do me a *favor* and show up right at my workplace."

"I can explain, but now isn't the time."

She crossed her arms. "Of course it isn't. Looks like you're doing fine. Probably been working out and partying with your friends in Vancouver?"

"You could say that." How the hell could he make her leave? "I know this is gonna sound weird, but something big is about to go down and you can't stay here."

Skepticism practically drenched her face, but when he didn't blink, she scanned the customers in the room. She assessed them with a trained eye, like her werewolf hunter father. "The rowdy boys in big coats or the folks in designer stuff?"

He chuffed. "Both? If one opens fire, the other ones will jump in."

Her dark eyebrows rose. "Are they all after *you*? Why?"

Time's running out, McGinnis.

He was practically ready to escape, but he had to get her out of there first.

"It's a long story, and no, just the fellows sitting to the left of me," he replied.

"What are they packing?"

Did she seriously just ask that?

In his peripheral vision, the rich lady whispered to one of her cohorts. The guard leaned her way, then he looked in Zach's direction. No, not Zach. The man was staring at Lark.

Why?

Hackles raised, Zach whispered, "You're leaving in thirty seconds."

She slowly shook her head in disbelief. "There are a bunch of innocent people in the kitchen."

"Those guys will shoot first and ask questions later, Lark."

Their gazes locked.

She hesitated, then nodded. "I'll try to get the high schoolers out of the kitchen."

Watching her retreating back should've filled him with hope, but regret sucker-punched him in the chest. Letting her go would save her life again. If he left her behind once, he could do it again.

Zach's grip on the handgun tightened, and he released the safety. Briefly, he closed his eyes and inhaled. Scents and sounds coursed over him. The important noises bled through the heavy bass and drums from Mountain singing "Mississippi Queen."

"No matter what," his good friend and alpha werewolf Kaden Windham told him, *"your senses are hyperaware now. Use them. Feel them."*

His fingertips itched. Claws always hurt when they emerged, but the hunger to fight fed adrenaline into his system.

The clinking of the dishes in the back kitchen ceased. Footsteps echoed and the sounds of Lark whispering to the staff reached his ears.

"Take fifteen," she said to them. "I'll take over for now."

She was telling the kids to take a break. Good.

"Why don't you rest for a bit, Dan?" she asked someone else back there.

"Naw, we got a big order from those dudes."

"Fine," she grumbled. But Zach didn't hear the back door open and close again.

What the hell? Why did she stay?

In the corner, Old Bart unbuttoned his coat. The barrel-chested man always carried the most heat. Fuck. Time was up. But to Zach's surprise, Old Bart pulled out a shotgun and aimed the weapon at Zach's head. The second his finger squeezed the trigger, Zach dropped to the ground, then launched himself over the counter.

As Zach landed hard on the tile floor, he sensed movement from the mysterious lady and her men. The burly guards tossed their table onto its side to guard their mistress.

From behind the counter, Zach caught the sounds of more gunfire and overturned tables.

Cops would be here soon. And damn it, Lark better be out of here.

He hurried to the end of the counter, away from the Red hunting clan and closer to the rich lady's party. The swinging door to the kitchen was a few feet away. At the far end, he peeked around the corner, tensing up to rush toward the nearest window.

He caught quite the sight. Instead of cowering, the woman kneeled behind the table and lifted her hands as if in the middle of prayer. Bullets pinged from the Red clan's guns and whizzed past her, but none of them touched her. The woman's lips quivered as she spoke in a language he didn't recognize. Suddenly, the ground shook beneath his feet. The windows rattled from some unseen force.

"What's going on?" one of the clan members said.

"Dunno. This ain't right," Old Bart replied. "V-formation. Eliminate them to *kill* to the wolf."

The Red hunting clan surged toward the woman's party, raining bullets on them while the guards returned fire.

Caught in the middle, Zach tensed up and prepared to run. Even if they filled him with silver bullets, he was getting the hell out of here.

~

SHOTS FIRED THROUGH THE DINING ROOM.

But that wasn't all—the earth trembled as if an earthquake had hit.

The shaking increased, erupting into a deafening roar from the dining area. The swinging door to the dining room opened and scalding air swept into the kitchen. An explosion flung Lark into the wall. Glass, pots, and pans rained down. Her breath rushed out of my lungs. Her ears rang.

Just when she thought the worst had passed, something heavy struck the side of her head. Bile rose in her throat as lights danced across her eyes.

With her face planted against the cold floor, all she could make out were screams and sparks from broken lights. The stench of smoke and burnt food seared her lungs. Blackness crept around the edge of her thoughts as her senses dulled.

Get up, damn it! she could hear her dad yell. He'd died less than a year ago, but his voice was still strong within her. *You're in danger, girl.*

In the past, she always got up. A dead DeStefano was the one who rested on their laurels. But her limbs refused to comply. Not far to her left, she heard the crunch of footsteps against the broken glass. Her heartbeat matched the throbbing pain in her head as it quickened.

Was Zach still out there?

She hoped until warm hands touched the top of her head and back. But their touch wasn't gentle. She caught a whiff of lavender, delicate and airy. The hands on her body didn't search for injuries or whisper words to soothe her pain. Heat spread from the feminine hands into her back. What the hell was going on?

Giovanni DeStefano had refused to teach Lark his hunting clan ways, but she'd listened when members of the Azzuro hunting clan from Sicily visited her dad's pub.

They spoke fervently of their cause. How the hunters must eliminate the wolves. None of those hunters would go down without a fight. Survivors didn't lie there.

So she tried to speak, but her mouth refused to cooperate. She willed her eyes to open. For her hands to clench into fists so she could strike the woman who pressed her cheek into the icy floor. The hands suddenly withdrew as another thunderous burst of flame engulfed the room, raising the temperature from tepid to scorching. Everything burned. Her back. Her lungs.

She'd died and gone to hell.

Why couldn't her head turn to see the woman? She wanted to see her attacker's face. Not that she could fight or spit at the woman, but something inside made her want to confront them. But she wouldn't have her chance. Darkness spread into her vision as she resisted the current toward the void.

A woman's voice bled into the dimness.

"A circle is a path with no ending and no beginning. You follow the circle now," the woman whispered to her. "No matter how winding the journey, you will never divert from where you need to be."

The fury Lark reached for never surfaced. As she fell unconscious, the fading warmth on her back spread across her chest, settling into an itch that coiled and tightened.

~

A white-hot explosion slammed Zach into the wall. The counter absorbed most of the force, but his entire chest screamed in agony. Debris from the ceiling rained down on him, blanketing him with tiles and glass.

He sucked in a smoke-filled breath, cringing as his flesh healed and knotted itself back together. He surmised he'd never get used to the peculiar feeling.

The sounds of bullets—like pelting rain—had ceased. Tactical body armor wouldn't protect the Red clan from an attack like that. Had the party on the other side of the room survived the blast?

Then a singular thought hit him hard: *Find Lark.*

He rolled onto his stomach and caught the scent of burning flesh. *Burnt wolf.* With a grunt, he ignored the pain and forced himself to rise. Through the smoke and building heat, he couldn't make out much. Only the faint wail of an oncoming siren bled through the roar of the fire.

Zach drew in a deep breath and held it. Not a single scent. He crept away from the counters to the back of the diner. A support beam blocked his entry, but with a mighty heave, he hoisted it out of the way. An entire section of the wall had collapsed—blown to bits by an unseen force. The last thing he'd seen was the woman in the white dress kneeling, her fists clenching as if she was preparing to punch a hole through the universe.

Had she attacked everyone instead?

Please be alive, Lark.

He wanted to see Lark again so he could find out why she'd stubbornly stayed.

Flames engulfed the kitchen. Thick smoke forced him to crouch. He ambled around the dented prep tables, over the scattered food on the floor. Finally, he caught a moan and spotted a figure leaning over another. It was the woman in white. How had she entered the kitchen so quickly? The woman he searched for lay at her feet.

Had she hurt Lark?

Fury gathered in him. A growl formed in his chest.

Leaping over fallen tables, he rushed to Lark. The woman in white glanced at him over her shoulder and then hurried out the open back door into the night.

He knelt next to Lark. Was she dead? He reached for her and caught a faint pulse—her heartbeat defiantly hammered in her chest.

Leave now, assess later.

Any minute now, the gas lines might ignite. They weren't safe here. Zach picked up Lark and carried her out the same door.

He searched the alley for the woman in white, but she'd vanished.

[2]

A persistent twitch on Lark's back drew her from slumber into the reality of a monstrous headache. The pain stabbed into her forehead like shards of glass. The early-morning sunlight smacking her face didn't help either.

A strong antiseptic smell filled the air. She was in a hospital. Heaven forgive her, she hated this fucking place. She attempted to sit up and winced from pain.

A rough night, indeed.

She tried to wrap her mind around the last thing she remembered, but every effort resulted in pain. Slowly, she brushed her fingertips against her aching forehead. As she examined the bandage binding her head, her fingers tangled in the wads of disheveled hair caught within the folds. How did she get here? The last thing she remembered was trying to get the damn cook out of the kitchen and seeing Zach for the first time in a long time.

She frowned as if she'd tasted something bad. Of course Zach would waltz back into her life and everything went to hell. And who were those guys hunting him? Maybe he'd pissed off some freelancers. Those for-hire mercenaries never liked to play by the hunting clans' rules.

The twitching slid down Lark's back, interrupting her thoughts. The quiver was so subtle that she assumed her hospital gown scratched against a sore spot. Her skin again tugged with a rippling tickle.

What the fuck was that?

Hospital gowns didn't move while their wearer held still. Horrified that she had squashed a bug, she patted the bed around her. No bugs. She ignored the pain while she checked her hospital gown. A fleck of bright red on her shoulder made her pause. Under the folds of her gown, she found a brilliant, multicolored snake tattoo embracing her naked curves.

She'd definitely hit her head—hard.

With a choked gasp, she eased off the bed. Not a smart move on her part. Pain sliced from the top of her head down to her neck while she disconnected herself from the heart monitor.

She had to see it.

Somehow, she pulled the IV stand to the bathroom. Even with the pain, she couldn't get there fast enough. The cold tile floor sent a chill from her feet up her legs, but she had to *see*. She had to know. A mirror never lied.

And there it was.

In the small confines of the bathroom, she gaped as her eyes followed the snake's body from her shoulder to her chest, where its head began on her left breast. The glossy blood-red head, with amber eyes, was the size of her closed fist. From the snake's position wrapped around her torso, she assumed the serpent spanned down her back to coil around her waist. Vivid scales in green, yellow, and crimson continued to roll around her hips across the top of her buttocks, and ended on her left thigh.

Yep, I've lost my damn mind, she thought.

Her hand began to shake. "Shit. Shit. Shit."

This had to be some cruel, elaborate joke.

Lark rubbed her fingers on the tattoo, expecting the skin to be sensitive or show signs of healing, as if it had maliciously been inked during her lost time. Yet her skin's texture where the serpent's head lay was unnaturally smoother and softer, like a baby's cheek. Not tender. As if the tattoo had been on her body for years. Her breath quickened, and her brain dimmed.

Maybe it's not real. Perhaps the bump on her head had left her crazier than her uncle Vincent after a bad pub party. She rubbed again, vigorously attempting to erase the ink buried under her skin.

"I have to be high as hell…" She had to find out exactly how she'd gotten here. Where did this tattoo come from? How had she gotten it? As she plodded back to her bed, she glanced at the door, as if expecting someone to rush into the room with spiteful intent.

The sooner she left the hospital, the sooner she could search for answers. But right now she needed some pain medication. The tattoo shifted again as she curled up on the bed. A quick peek down her gown made her reluctant to learn anything.

After a few knocks, a short and cheerful nurse opened the door and appeared. "Glad to see you finally woke up. How are you feeling?"

Lark opened her mouth, then closed it again. Yeah, she'd settle for a sane question first. Asking a nurse about a moving tattoo was loco. "How did I get here?"

"Well, sweetie, you were with several patients from the diner attack around midnight last night." The nurse jotted some notes in Lark's chart. "You're lucky the worst of your injuries is a concussion, along with some scrapes and bruises. The majority of the patients are in the ICU."

Oh, no.

The nurse glanced at the monitor she'd reattached to Lark's hand. "Your pulse is elevated. Do you need some pain meds?"

A head injury and a pounding headache were the *least* of Lark's problems right now. "Are there any men in the ICU? The head cook?" Zach's name sat on the tip of her tongue, but she didn't mention him. He had probably abandoned ship again and was back in Vancouver sleeping the night off.

"I can't tell you that. Rest first. I'm sure you'll find out soon enough." The nurse gave her a sympathetic smile and patted her arm. "You have a concussion and minor burns, but that's about it. You need to calm down and get some rest. I'll let the resident physician know you're up. He can tell you more about your condition."

She turned to leave but paused at the door. "By the way, Dr. Mills and the nurses' station are buzzing about your tattoo. That probably took months to get done."

"No time at all," Lark mumbled. Good God, at least that meant she wasn't delusional about the tat.

"Well, get some rest and we'll check on you later." At the doorway, the nurse dimmed the lights, and the shadows in the room deepened.

After the nurse left, Lark stared at the door. Any minute now, she expected it to open, and for some semblance of reality to march inside.

But she was lying on a hospital bed instead of waking up around lunchtime to do a zombie shuffle to her next job at a vegan cafeteria.

She took in the IV connected to her arm and the rest of her private room. Not only did she have her own bathroom, but a sitting area, too. There was no way she could afford all this stuff, much less the bills from all the specialists. Who the hell had told them she should be in here?

The open door to the bathroom slowly swung toward her. How long had someone hid behind there? A sliver of fear danced down her spine. Lark reached for the nearest weapon —anything would do—and grasped a remote. The cheap plastic made poor walloping material.

A figure emerged from behind the door, and she threw the remote in disgust.

Zach snatched the remote in midair.

Out of all the people to show up…again.

"Patients shouldn't be throwing things," he said.

She counted to ten, for his *safety*, before she spoke. "What are you doing here?"

He rolled his eyes. "Visiting hours aren't until after ten."

"So you just snuck in?" She gave him a dark look.

"I've been in and out of the room since last night."

Heavy footsteps echoed outside the door. Lark froze and glanced at the door, expecting the doctor to show up, but no one did.

Zach didn't so much as twitch.

Lark eased back onto the sheets as a wave of dizziness hit. Bile tickled the back of her throat, but she refused to vomit.

He took a step closer. Now he filled far too much space, and she wanted to sink further into the covers.

"You shouldn't have gotten up earlier." A glimmer of the old Zach crossed his face as a small smile touched his features.

As the nausea passed, she tried to glare at him, but doing that hurt too, so she gave up. Staying mad at a guy like Zach wasn't easy.

His features had sharpened, but Zach always had the most expressive eyes. A quirky grin and jokes galore that lightened the saddest of moments. When he laughed, light brown flecks appeared in his irises. This man, who wore a long, dark coat, had an edge to him the old Zach didn't have.

Had something bad happened to him since she'd last seen him?

"I got up because I had to see something…" She held her breath while she considered what to say next.

Right now, she didn't trust him as far as she could throw him. Less than a year ago, she would've trusted him with her life. In a hospital room, similar to the one she was lying in now, she'd cried with him and prayed with him for her father's life. Prostate cancer had ravaged his body. While in another room, not far down the hall, his older sister Cynthia received treatment for her leukemia. Zach and Lark were the walking dead, stumbling from room to room, trying to figure out why their loved ones had been marked for death.

Right now, she needed that man. She squeezed her eyes shut and sighed. Hadn't he known loss intimately since his hunter parents disappeared when he was a kid? She knew the same loss. Werewolves had killed her mother when she was ten. Hadn't he hungered for retribution too, since he lived as a werewolf hunter?

Both of them knew death intimately.

"I woke up with this tattoo." Reluctantly, she drew her hospital gown down, stopping just before the top of her breast. The head of the serpent rested there.

His jaw twitched. "You do have a concussion. Maybe you forgot about it."

She snorted. "This one is *everywhere*. Believe me, I wouldn't forget hours and hours of sitting in a chair to get this sucker done." The hairs on the back of her neck rose. "She did something to me…"

Zach stood like a sentinel beside her, not reflecting her rising fear.

"Before I blacked out," she murmured, "I remember

someone pressing my face against the floor. Then a tightening sensation all over while she said something weird about circles and paths."

His brow knotted as if he considered her words. "None of this sounds good."

He strode to the nearby window and peeked through the blinds. Light from the rising sun illuminated part of his face before he returned to her bedside. "You're sweating profusely. Should I call the nurse?"

He reached for the call button next to her bed, but she stopped him.

"How did she give me a *tattoo*?" she whispered. "Shit, maybe I should be asking if she was the one who caused the explosion—"

"It was her," he said.

"Damn. Really weird."

"Oh yeah." He folded his arms. "When you were sleeping last night, I tried to track her, but she disappeared at the end of the alley behind the diner."

"Maybe someone picked her up?"

"Maybe."

A knock on the door made her jump. She turned to Zach, but all she caught was the faint yawn of the bathroom door swinging to obscure Zach behind it. Damn, he moved faster than a high school boyfriend getting caught in his girlfriend's bedroom.

An older, bald doctor in scrubs entered the room. "Your nurse told me you're up, so I thought I'd come and check on you."

She read the embroidered name of Dr. Mills on his white coat. Under that, she caught the name of the hospital: University of Washington Medical Center.

So that was where she'd ended up.

"Nice to meet you," she managed to say.

She peeked around the doctor, but Zach remained silent.

The doctor checked her vitals and asked her the standard questions. Everything he said blended together until he gave her instructions to rest for the day. "Your concussion was pretty severe, Lark. I'll prescribe some Zofran for the nausea and we'll observe you for the next couple of hours. If you improve, you should be well enough to go home tomorrow. Can someone pick you up?"

"Yeah, my aunt Gretchen can drive down from Vancouver."

"Sounds like a good plan." The doctor said his goodbyes and left the room.

The moment the doctor was gone, Zach reappeared. He edged toward the closed door and waited.

Was something wrong?

"We can't stay here," he said, his voice low.

"Excuse me?"

"While the doctor was examining you, some women passed your room. They spoke to the staff at the nurses' station."

"And? Isn't this a hospital?"

"One of them said they were searching for their sister. They said she could be identified by her *snake tattoo.*"

A sliver of ice slid down the middle of her back.

Sister, my ass.

If her family had heard about her hospitalization, her uncles would've rolled down here ready to rumble, but who would know she had a tattoo? She wanted off this merry-go-round right now.

"I wonder if the woman who attacked the diner is back," she whispered. "I wish I knew who she was."

"I don't know, but I suspect she's dangerous."

Their gazes locked, and the intensity of his made her heartbeat quicken. She forced herself to look away.

"The best option is for you to leave," he said. "I could go out there and confront them, but we're in a hospital."

"And patients could get caught in the crossfire." She sighed. "Pop always wanted me to stay out of hunter business. Maybe an old Azzurro hunting clan enemy has come calling."

His eyes darkened. "This feels *much* deadlier than hunter business."

~

ZACH WATCHED HER CHEST RISE AND FALL WITH hitched breaths. The scent of her fear permeated the air.

He glanced at the door again.

Why was he still here? Hadn't he walked away from her less than a year ago to protect her from the world of the werewolves and hunters?

Last night, he'd made a grave mistake. He'd walked into the diner with his enemies not far behind him and brought his mess to Lark's workplace.

As he gazed at Lark sitting on the bed, with her shoulders slumped and her brow knitted with pain, he couldn't walk away. The threat outside wasn't from werewolves or their hunters, but from something neither of them understood. He wouldn't let her stand alone.

Once she's safe, I can run again, he reminded himself. *Maybe disappear into the Canadian wilderness. She doesn't need to know what I've…become.*

Before he left her behind for good, he'd find out what was wrong with her. She didn't smell the same. Usually, Lark carried a faint citrus scent—it was the shampoo she used— but this morning, other than the faint black licorice odor that he'd learned meant pain and exhaustion, an unfamiliar scent wafted from her. It was an herbal one he'd never smelled before.

"I know you're tired, but I fear for your safety," he whispered, listening for sounds in the hallway.

"You heard them, but you didn't *see* them. Maybe they're not a threat." She eased off the side of the bed.

He hated seeing her like this, covered in bruises and wincing as if she'd high-fived a Mack truck at full speed. She should be back in Vancouver finishing her master's degree in biochemistry—not working at some diner.

"We should know what you're up against before we let them in," he said. "It's better to meet your enemy on the high ground." He reached for her to brush strands of her hair out of her face, but stopped himself. They weren't like that anymore.

"You sound like my dad," she grumbled.

From his inner coat pocket, he plucked out a maroon shirt and a pair of shorts. He'd guessed her size when he bought them from the gift shop.

She read the sappy get-well-soon quote on the front of the shirt and gave him a smothered chuckle. "How come you don't look as fucked up as I do right now?" Her gaze swept over him with a stern eye. "Not a single scratch."

He turned away from her as if he could hide what he'd become. Yeah, right. "I was behind the counter during the explosion. I guess I got lucky."

She gingerly reached around her waist to release her hospital gown ties.

"Here, let me help," he offered.

"No, I got it." She fumbled a couple times and cursed. "No, I don't."

Reluctantly, she leaned forward, and he untied the ties— only to stop cold. The massive tattoo she'd described stretched over her right shoulder and wrapped twice over her upper back. The snake's multicolored scales reflected the overhead lights.

"It's creepy," he said.

Real tattoos didn't have special effects.

He checked out the only familiar ink he recognized: the profile of a horned lark on her left shoulder.

Mom's favorite bird, she'd revealed to him after a late night of pizza and drinking. Lark didn't have many tats—just the lark on her back, a hummingbird on her right hip, and a raven on her ankle.

"The snake…moves, too," she said faintly. "First werewolves are real. Now moving tattoos are on the menu. I'm scared to think of what else is out there."

You and me both, he thought.

Lark shifted away from him. While she put on her shirt, he gave her some privacy. He hungered to see if she was well —while other parts of him wanted to see if her skin was as smooth as it felt the last time he touched her.

Not now, McGinnis. Save the dame first.

"It's gonna be story time around the campfire for both of us," she added as she pulled on the shorts. Once she was dressed, she said, "It's cold as hell outside, Z. Should I waltz out of here in shorts and a shirt?"

"You're going to wear my coat." He handed it off, and the garment swallowed her. Carefully, he drew the hood over her head. When he was satisfied she was bundled up, he helped her into a pair of slippers from the hospital.

His long-sleeve black wool shirt and jeans should help him avoid suspicion.

"Did they save any of my stuff?" she asked.

He glanced into the cubby next to the bed and found nothing. "The hospital probably locked away any valuables you had in your pockets."

"I can get my ID later. My purse was probably a burnt, soggy mess back at the diner."

He went to the door, paused, and listened. There were no sounds of approaching hospital workers. Only the persistent beeps and chirps of hospital machinery in other rooms.

"Is something wrong?" Lark asked from behind him.

"We're good. Keep the hood on until we get to the stairwell."

They crept through the door and ambled down the hallway. He caught the light footsteps of an approaching nurse and directed Lark into a dark, empty room. Once the path was clear again, they hurried to the nearest stairwell. When he caught her increased heart rate and quickened breath, he slowed down a bit.

If she collapsed, they'd have bigger problems to tackle.

He gently pushed her to sit on the stairs. "How you holding up?"

"Like somebody used a jackhammer on the back of my head."

Unable to stop himself, he touched the gauze wrapped around her head. Had the woman in white hurt her? If he encountered that woman again, she had answers to give, or she'd face his fury.

"I'm ready now." Lark tried to stand, but he maneuvered her to sit again. The warmth of her skin seeped into him, and his breath caught as a strange tingling sensation fluttered along his fingertips.

That was unexpected.

"We're not safe here," she whispered.

"No, we're not, but if I have to, I'll carry you out of here."

Lark pursed her lips. "You're not carrying me anywhere."

He rubbed his face in irritation. She held a grudge like no other. "If you're hurt, I might not have a choice."

Lark rose and gave an annoyed groan. Now that made him smile. She shuffled past him and headed down the stairwell.

Once they reached the first floor, he took point again. "Don't look at anyone and stay behind me."

"You got a car?"

He chuckled. "No, we're gonna escape with my bus pass."

Pedestrians and patients filled the first floor of the hospital. Lark and Zach weaved past them, their heads turned down and stride quickened.

Close to the doors, Zach sensed a pair of eyes on their backs. But their trail didn't smell like his crew. Whoever they were, they'd used soap and deodorant. After hunting him for the past couple of months, the Red hunters could've used a shower or two.

The brisk November wind whipped against Zach's face, but the cold didn't bother him anymore. Lark's legs were bare, so he led her quickly to a black sedan in the parking lot.

After they were safely inside, she said, "This is nice. I thought you liked trucks."

He started the car, and soon they slipped out of the lot. "I prefer trucks, but right now I don't have the option to be picky."

She gave him a long look, and he could practically hear the questions: what was he doing back in Seattle? Who was hunting him?

Above all, he dreaded telling her he wasn't human anymore. Lark had a solid head on her shoulders. But as the daughter of a hunter, all she'd heard was the standard propaganda: werewolves hunted and killed innocent humans.

He'd had the same upbringing, but Lark's dad hadn't trained her to be a hunter from the crib like his parents had.

"Where are we going?" she asked.

He released the breath he held. He still had time to figure

out what to say. "There's an old Red hunting clan hideout nearby in Coalfield. We'll be safer outside of Seattle."

"A hunter hideout? Didn't you say some freelancers were chasing you earlier?"

So she thought some freelancers were after him. Those mercs were everywhere and did anything for a buck. "We don't have a lot of choices. A hideout will have weapons, food, and supplies."

For thirty minutes, they drove southeast. Zach tried to focus on the road, but the familiar sights settled into his bones. Good ole Seattle. He'd lived here before. His parents had taken him back and forth over the Evergreen Point Bridge they crossed right now. The McGinnises had hunted for prey in Bellevue. Chased down werewolves on Mercer Island. The gigs in Seattle had lined the McGinnises' pockets —but prey migrated to new havens, and, like all hunting groups, they had to follow.

Skyscrapers and civilization became forests of pine and elm. The four-lane highway switched to two lanes. Beside him, Lark rested her head against the window. Her breath fogged the glass. The need to draw her close to him tugged at him, but he clenched the steering wheel tighter instead.

They were almost to Coalfield. Soon enough, she could rest and he could guard her and keep his distance.

On the way, they passed an exit leading to Factoria. His family had lived there, too. Damn, he missed that place. He vividly recalled the day when his parents had packed up their things and dragged their three young kids with them. His younger brother, Ty, hated moving, while Cynthia, his steadfast older sister, helped his mom and dad pack.

"You need to stop getting used to our houses," Cyn had said to him. *"A home is made up of the people who live in it."* She was always the strong one, leading the way and forcing a bunch of little kids to be hunters like their parents.

He'd have to find a new home now.

The hideout he'd mentioned was an old house on the outskirts of Coalfield. The place wasn't a town, per se, more like a neighborhood right outside of Renton to the west. Trees obscured many of the houses, providing privacy from the road. The Red hunting clan had bought the property twenty years ago after a wolf pack had settled here for the summer.

They pulled up in front of the single-story gray shingle house. The neighborhood was quiet, with few houses nearby. Patches of dead grass on the lawn told him that a hunter hadn't been by here recently for upkeep. Dark curtains obscured the inside from behind the bar-covered windows. Dirt and leaves littered the doorstep.

Perfect.

"We should be safe here for a little while," he said. "Do you have anyone you need to call?"

"Yeah, my uncle will be worried."

He gave her a phone. "I got a backup I can charge. That way you can check in with your family while I figure out who was trailing you at the hospital."

He checked for danger first. This time of the morning, most folks had left home. The street was quiet, and he hoped things stayed that way.

They left the car. At the house, he found the keys under the fourth loose shingle off the side of the structure. Once the door was unlocked, they hurried inside. A heavy, musty odor hit him, but he welcomed the smell. That meant no one had been inside for a while. Layer after layer of dust coated the dated furniture in the living room, but the windows had bars and the heater should work. Hopefully.

"Wait here while I sweep the house," he said.

"I'll make those calls, then."

"Call your family, but—"

"Don't tell them where I'm at. I'm not a newbie, Z."

He made his way to the thermostat and cranked up the heat, all the while trying not to listen to her conversation.

"I had a feeling you saw the news, Uncle Vincent, so I called you first. I didn't want auntie to worry." Her footsteps echoed on the wooden floor from the living room to the kitchen. She chatted a bit longer, then hung up to make another call.

Who else did she need to call? A boyfriend?

"Hey, Tess. I'm okay. I'm okay," she said softly. "Yeah, I have a feeling the whole place was trashed. Have you called the insurance company yet?"

While he gathered the house's first-aid kit—just in case she needed it—he faintly caught the sounds of an older woman through the phone. Maybe the diner's owner. The two chatted about her coworkers' condition and how Lark planned to lie low with her uncle in Vancouver for a couple of weeks.

"I'm in no condition to work anyway," she murmured.

He wondered what she meant. He needed to ask her what she was doing in Seattle in the first place. Didn't she have a life and family back in Vancouver?

A couple of minutes passed, and the house fell silent. When he returned to the living room and placed a pair of scissors and the kit on the coffee table, he noticed she'd removed the cover from the couch. Now she lay on top, curled up on her side. At first, he stood rooted to his spot behind her, not wanting to disturb her rest. But his hungry gaze drank her in. From the top of her head to her legs peeking out from under the coat. The garment obscured her curves, but he remembered her well. Memories of touching her pulsed through him.

Hadn't they used to make out at every opportunity? At first, she'd admitted spending time with him was a way for her to forget her troubles, but the spark between them was undeniable.

Back then.

Maybe that was why it hurt like hell to leave.

She's still mine, the wolf within him whispered. The possessive feeling startled him, and he tried to ignore it.

Walk away, his heart warned him. He could sit next to the door and listen for danger. Hell, he could pick up his phone and browse the web for intel on legends about moving tattoos.

And yet he couldn't force himself to look away. Damn, he'd missed her. He'd missed her laugh. He'd even missed the wry replies and sour looks she gave him when she didn't like what he had to say.

He shifted to head to the door, then Lark shivered. She curled up to tuck her legs into the coat, but she was too tall. With a swallowed curse, he grabbed the couch cover. A hard yank cleared out most of the dust. He drew the cover over her.

There, nice and easy.

Her eyes briefly opened, then closed again.

Zach hesitated, then sat and drew his arm under her shoulder to arrange her so that her head rested against his left thigh and she lay comfortably on the couch.

Lark stiffened but tolerated his presence.

All he had to do was sit there and guard her, but every nerve ending within his stomach fired.

To quench his need to touch her, he placed his hand on her shoulder. He flexed his fingers to offer comfort, but the bare skin from her neck to her cheekbone called to him. After hesitating twice, he finally traced the curve of her cheek. So soft. So smooth.

She relaxed against him as he stroked her skin. The wrinkles in her brow washed away.

With Lark's heartbeat steady and her breath slowing from sleep, the tension in his stomach eased and he laid his head back—right as a delicious sensation rippled under his fingertips and warmed her skin. He glanced down at Lark to see a hint of a smile on her lips.

If touching her would always feel this good, he'd do it all the time.

His smile faded when he watched a dark bruise lighten on the back of her neck.

No way.

Was that him? When he withdrew his hand, the honeyed sensation ceased, only to begin again when he stroked her face.

He stopped and took in his palm. Lark turned to look at him. Their gazes connected, and realization hit him hard as she looked from his hand to his face.

"What did you do to me?" She rubbed the spot with the lightened bruise.

He reached for her, but she sat up and jerked away from him.

"I'm not sure," he admitted.

"You healed me," she whispered.

He swallowed deeply. A year ago, he hadn't believed the rumor that a few alpha werewolves could heal—until Kaden had healed him. But Zach wasn't an alpha. He had no pack either, yet the impossible had occurred.

The silence between them stretched out to painful levels.

He searched her wide eyes, seeing the pieces fall in place in her head: from how his appearance had changed to how he'd survived the explosion without a scratch.

And now he'd dropped another bomb in this room.

"When did you plan to tell me you became a werewolf?" she whispered, her voice dark and hollow.

[3]

Zach watched her wobble to stand, but he didn't interfere. He let her add distance between them. If she collapsed, though, all bets were off.

Lark retreated to the dining room and slumped into the closest seat. Even from the other side of the room, her fear-heavy scent slammed into him. He knew she'd strike him if he stepped forward, so he held still.

"Answer me," she said. "You're not the same."

His body tensed up, and he prepared himself for the onslaught. He deserved it.

"You're stronger. Less lanky." She examined him from afar, as if there was another sign for her to see. "You're *feral* in a way you weren't before."

"I'm still Zach," he said.

"You're one of *them*. You're one of the lowlifes that killed my mom." The strength in her voice weakened, and he could see the furrows in her brow as the pain from her concussion returned. The urge to reach for her and touch her grew painful. Was it the wolf within him that wanted to heal her again?

No, I still care about her. Walking away to protect her hadn't changed that.

"Why would you do such a *vile* thing to yourself?" she added.

"Does it matter?"

"Yes, it does."

He approached her and sat on the floor where the living room ended and the dining room began. He left enough space between them that if she fainted, he'd be close enough to catch her. "A lot has happened since you and I last saw each other."

"No shit. The Zach McGinnis I knew was a dedicated hunter. He wouldn't become a werewolf unless he was *forced* to become one."

He let out a long breath. "I had a change of heart."

She scooted her seat away from him. "A change of heart? I'd rather die."

He could've chosen death—but he'd decided to live. Not all werewolves were bad, but he'd had to learn that after one saved both his life and his sister's.

"Do you remember my sister Cyn?" he asked. "All this began with her."

She didn't speak for a bit. Finally, she said, "Yeah, I remember Cynthia. Is she…still alive?" Lark was still pissed, but at least she'd replied.

"Alive and well." Zach unburdened himself. He started with how he'd met Kaden Windham while Cyn was sick in the hospital. How he'd struck a deal: if Kaden saved his dying sister's life, Zach would agree to protect the Windham Pack sanctuary in the mountains outside of Vancouver.

In order to accomplish the near-impossible feat, Zach had left Lark behind and whisked Cynthia away from the hospital to Kaden's cabin. After that, he kept his eye on Red hunting clan activity and monitored the sanctuary border to keep freelancers away. Everything had gone as planned until another hunting clan swept in and drove the Windhams south. After all the fighting, the Windhams had eventually settled in Montana.

Cyn's new family was safe. For now.

But he'd left Lark behind to do all this.

"You *gave* her to a wolf?" she said quietly. "Are you out of your mind?"

"Yeah, I was desperate. She was dying." He swallowed the lump that formed in the back of his throat every time he recalled Cyn lying in the middle of the bed, her skin pale and eyes void of life. "You know how chemotherapy works. The cocktail *and* the cancer kill you. It was either throw a Hail Mary and hope for success or watch her wither away like…"

"Like my father?" Lark finished. Slowly, she turned away from him to stare at the wall.

He didn't say a word. He could've dragged Giovanni to Kaden's cabin too, but Lark's dad would've killed himself before he let a werewolf touch him.

Tension rose to uncomfortable levels in the room, but he didn't speak. What could he say? Nothing would change the past, and if he had the choice again, he'd still send his sister to Kaden.

"Your sister is a hunter. A damn good one," Lark finally whispered as if deep in thought. "I'm surprised she didn't try to kill Kaden."

Zach stifled a laugh. "Kaden can handle himself, but I'm sure Cyn tried to kill him a couple of times."

"And what about you?" He sensed her eyes on him. "How did you become one of them?"

"My hunting clan didn't exactly approve of what I did for Cyn and the Windhams." His hands formed fists and he forced himself to unclench them. So much had gone down. So many people hurt in the aftermath.

"They marked you for death."

"And they almost finished the job in Montana. I was near dead when I crossed Kaden's doorstep. He's a doctor and all, but my injuries were beyond his care or his ability to heal me. I had to make a choice: live on as a werewolf or die as a human."

He left the rest of the story in the air, since his current circumstances had serendipitously led him to Lark's diner.

For the longest time, she said nothing. The only sound in the room was the hum from the fridge. The periodic whine of the heater kicking in.

"You can be mad at me all you want, but I did what I had to do—" he began.

"We all have free will. I just wished you hadn't made the choices you did."

Zach nodded faintly. "Even if I had stayed, your dad didn't want me around. He told me I'd endanger you sooner or later."

"Sounds like him."

"He told me he'd rise from the dead to hunt me if I hurt you," he murmured.

Just walk out the door. Giovanni DeStefano had told him from his deathbed. *You don't want to watch her die like I did my Lupita.*

The present tugged him back to Lark and they sat in silence until she spoke.

"I'm certain someone targeted me at the diner," Lark said. "I don't know who is behind all this, but I need answers."

"Yes, you do," he agreed.

She rubbed her hands together. He recognized the gesture—Lark only did that when she had to make choices she didn't like. "And I don't want to find them with you." She stood slowly. "In the morning, I'm going home. I want you to drop me off at the nearest train station. My uncles are too old to be dragged into this, so I'm going to crash back in Vancouver with some friends."

"Not a good idea."

"End of discussion," she snapped.

Frustration hit his gut. Did she really think she could run to some *friend's* apartment and hide from armed assailants?

"If you drag your friends into your mess, things won't end well," he murmured.

"I'm not Cyn." Her face was emotionless. "I don't need you to rescue me. You should've left me in that hospital this morning and walked away."

As hard as Lark tried to get some shuteye in the bedroom, her eyes kept popping open.

Exhaustion tugged at her senses, but her mind raced with the events of the last twenty-four hours. Visions of the serpent, the attack on the diner, and, finally, Zach's return ran through her noggin on repeat.

Too much, too quickly, her brain whined.

Before she knew it, she fell asleep and didn't awaken until light from the setting sun shone through the faded brown curtains on the window next to the bed.

Tentatively, she touched the gauze on her wound. The spot on the back of her head was still tender, but the area on her neck where Zach had healed her didn't hurt anymore. Matter of fact, she could turn her head without wincing.

Healing me doesn't make him a good guy, she reminded herself. He'd sacrificed his humanity to become one of *them.*

Lark rolled onto her side. She was in no hurry to get up and face the world outside. Tomorrow morning she'd have to ask Zach for that ride to the train station.

Her empty stomach grumbled. *Traitor.*

From her new position, she couldn't miss his scent within the folds of the garment she'd slept in. Before she crashed, she'd considered sleeping on the blankets, but the musty smell made her headache worse.

Damn him and his fine taste in soap. Didn't he say someone was chasing him? How come he didn't stink to high heaven? She shook her head with a wry grin.

The first time she'd met him, right outside of her dad's pub, it wasn't his dry humor that attracted him to her, but the cologne he wore. That December day was a cold one back in Vancouver. Members of the Azzurro hunting clan had gathered to drink and reminisce.

She'd left after her structural biology class on the University of Toronto campus to work a shift at the pub. On the way inside, she'd spotted several hunters chatting and smoking outside. If you've seen one menacing dude in fatigues, you've seen them all. All of their backs were turned to her, so she didn't bother to greet them—not that they didn't once holler at her, but facing Giovanni's wrath made many men give up easily.

As she passed them, a divine scent drew her attention. The tall stranger's cologne was subtle, with hints of cedar and sandalwood, yet the intoxicating smell slipped deliciously up her inner thighs and made her stop mid-step.

The dark-haired man turned around, and she came face to face with Zach.

"Hey," he'd said. Nothing smooth or cheesy to make her brush him off.

The words "Wow, you smell good enough to eat" came to mind, but she'd dated enough guys on campus to have some common sense. "What's up?"

"Nothing much."

The chilly wind whipped her hair into her mouth—you

know, the perfect timing to make your entrance less dramatic—and Zach brushed it out of her face.

It was that simple gesture that moved her. That singular moment in the past that made her hate herself for drawing her nose into Zach's hood to smell his cologne. She lingered here and there until she found that one spot that smelled the most like *him*.

She'd never forgotten about him, even as her grad school classes started up again in January. She thought she'd seen the last of him until he passed the pub during her late-night shifts.

Not once, but four times.

"Is he a stalker?" she recalled asking her dad.

He'd chuckled and patted her shoulder. "An excellent hunter knows when to make his move. Be patient."

Lark waited for Zach to come inside, maybe even to order a lager and say hello, but he never did. He was an ever-present shadow until she saw him again at the cancer center that early summer. Both of them were there to take their respective family member in for treatment.

And that was when their relationship had truly begun.

She inhaled again and sighed. When she had her fill and couldn't ignore her stomach anymore, she sat up. The movement made her a bit lightheaded, but she felt far better than the post-train-wreck feeling she'd had when she woke up this morning.

Time to find some chow.

As she rose to stand, the snake slid along her torso. The scales seemingly scratched her skin. *Ugh.* She'd never get used to that feeling. She waited for the strange sensation to end, but the tattoo shifted even more, as if it had decided camping out along the lower half of her body was ideal.

"You gotta be kidding me," she whispered. "Are you gonna do this shit every time I'm hungry?"

The compulsion to check the mirror in the master bathroom grew stronger and stronger. Just one glimpse this morning had been bad enough, but she couldn't take it anymore.

Lark shuffled across the room to the tiny bathroom on the other side. In three footsteps, she stood in the small bathroom before her reflection. She avoided touching herself and focused on seeing what gymnastics the tat was up to this time.

Gingerly, she pulled her shirt down by the collar. That pesky lizard no longer sat above her breast. Time to play hunt the tat. As carefully as possible, she slipped her arms out of the shirt holes and hiked the shirt over her shoulders. Now that the fabric hung around her neck, she could tilt her head to glance over her shoulder. The tattoo remained on her back, stark against her tanned skin. She shuddered as the serpent slid up her back again. The crimson head peeked over her other shoulder, blinking as the tongue darted in and out.

No freaking way.

In horror, she squeezed her eyes shut and clenched the sink to support her weakened legs. When she reopened her eyes, the tattoo remained, part of its body caressing her shoulder. Dark marks etched into its skin drew her gaze.

Foreign words materialized before her eyes. Like scratches carved in flesh, the words blinked from the other language into English.

CUSTODES TUI QUI TE EXSPECTAT. REPERIO COR TUUM IN RUINAS FLAMMA CONSUMSIT.

Your guardians are waiting for you. Find your heart's burnt ruins.

$$[\ 4 \ ]$$

"What the hell is that?" Zach said from behind her.

Lark glanced in the mirror to see him staring wide-eyed at her back.

She pulled down her shirt. "I don't know. A message." After learning about werewolves, one would think encountering magical moving tattoos wouldn't be as traumatizing, but at this point she'd settle for Black Death.

"Does it hurt?" he asked.

"No." She stared daggers at him. "Do you mind knocking before you barge inside?"

He raised his hands in surrender. "I heard you get up. When you didn't come out, I was worried you didn't feel well. I found you a pair of sweats and some sneakers in the supply closet."

She accepted the clothes. "Thanks for your concern, but I don't need your help anymore."

Zach grasped her shoulders and turned her to face him. He tilted her chin up.

She forced herself to take in his face. Would she see a monster hiding in there?

"Back when I first met you, you told me I needed to stop trying to save the world all the time. That one man couldn't do the work of many…and what did you call me?"

She tried not to smile but couldn't resist.

"I called you Captain Killjoy," she mumbled.

"What was that? I didn't hear you."

She frowned. He probably could hear her from across the street now.

She repeated what she said, much louder.

"So you remember," he said with a grin.

Back when she'd first met him at the pub, he was a rising star in the Red hunting clan, a man even her father respected, but he was too serious for a twenty-one-year-old. Most of the guys she met on campus partied late over the weekends.

But not Zach McGinnis.

The snake shifted along her stomach as the message on its skin fluttered through her mind again. But instead of a reminder, it was a *push* this time. What the hell?

Her gaze flitted to the bedroom door. Beyond that lay the living room and the front door. If she grabbed Zach's keys, she could go there—

"What are you thinking right now?" he asked, interrupting her thoughts.

"That I need to go to Dad's pub—what's left of it." The words slipped out of her mouth before she could snatch them back.

She hadn't returned to the bar since the day the insurance assessor had stopped by eight months ago. Who'd want to see their father's blood, sweat, and lifelong dream turned into a hollowed-out building?

"Now that my hunting days have ended, this place will feed

us," Dad had said. *"Someday, The Hunting Grounds will feed you, too."*

She could see the old pub vividly in her mind. Her dad had saved up the bounties from killing werewolves and bought the building not long after she was born. The property used to house a fly-by-night printing press before her father turned it into a neighborhood pub.

Zach slowly shook his head. "That could be a trap. Neither of us know what the hell that thing is. It could be killing you for all we know."

She scoffed. "I don't know what's going on, but this is the only opportunity I have for answers."

He sighed but didn't back up from her. Matter of fact, he took up far more space in the tiny bathroom than she preferred. Having Zach looming nearby didn't help. His presence reminded her of how easily her arms used to wrap around his waist. How her head rested perfectly against his chest.

But he was one of them now.

Like hell she'd let him hold her again.

Just because this mess fell into their laps didn't mean they should try to hook up again.

She'd tried to move on. First, she'd gone out with a study partner in her biotechnology class. He was too clingy. Then a construction foreman who lived in her apartment building asked her out—but never showed up to the second date.

At this point, her dating success rate needed first aid.

"Are you hungry?" Zach asked, finally ending the silence.

"I'm starving," she admitted.

"I'm going to get some food at the corner mart. I'll be back in fifteen. Get some sleep until I return." He left the bathroom but lingered near the bedroom door. "Promise me you won't leave until I return. We can plan things out together."

She sighed but nodded. She wouldn't get far on foot anyway.

As Zach left, the cold entered the room and retreated just as quickly.

She switched out the shorts for the sweatpants. Slipped on the shoes. Then she glanced at the wall clock in the living room. The dust-covered hands ticked along. *Tick. Tick. Tick.* Every minute that passed, the compulsion to go to the pub strengthened.

At first, she curled on her side on the couch, facing away from the clock. The serpent slid down her belly, creating an unnerving sensation.

She shuddered.

Yep, it's gonna take me some time to get used to that. Might be time to check out tattoo-removal establishments.

Twisting to her back on the couch, she drew the shirt up until her stomach was revealed. Bruises discolored spots here and there. Tentatively, she drew her finger along her lower ribs, working her way toward the tat near her navel. Before her very eyes, the tattoo slid away from her approaching hand.

Creepy as fuck.

She reached out and touched it, expecting a real snake to be there, but it was nothing more than her skin.

With a deep breath, she closed her eyes and tried to imagine the day before this one. How normal the day had gone. She snorted, recalling she'd need years and tons of cash to renovate The Hunting Grounds and get the place functional again.

There was no way in hell she could show up to a job in this condition.

An image of the bar crept into her head like an unsettling fog. She tried to shove the idea away and failed. Turning over to get some sleep was a futile gesture.

Might as well try to get up and get some water or something. She eased herself to stand and winced from head pain.

He could heal you, you know.

Lark slam-dunked that thought into the nearby trash. No way.

But a vicious werewolf hadn't whisked her away from danger this morning. He was the same man who'd held her while she bawled her eyes out and mourned her dad's illness.

Lark opened the ancient fridge and found a block of unidentifiable cheese. With all the mold growing on it, she couldn't even make out the manufacturer on the packaging. Gross.

She checked the window over the sink. An evening breeze tugged at the pine branches outside. Leaves gathered in messy, wet piles in the backyard. Some fresh air would be nice.

"You're facing north," a deathly quiet voice whispered in her mind. *"Just one hundred and forty miles from where you need to be."*

She shivered. Had she imagined hearing someone? She checked all the rooms but found no one.

After returning to the kitchen, convinced she'd imagined the voice, she found the window latch—quite rusted—and tugged on it until the fastener gave way. With a yank, she opened the window, and chilled air flooded the room.

The wind rustled her hair. Quite nice. Fresh air should make the hallucinations go away. She turned around and slumped against the counter until her bottom hit the floor. From there, she rested for a while.

Suddenly, the snake twitched. Not once, but three times. Then the serpent coiled tightly around her.

Something was wrong.

She waited in the kitchen, listening for sounds. Only the whisper of the heat through the vents filled the condo.

The compulsion to leave scratched at her throat over and over again. Her breath quickened and she blinked through a wave of pain.

What the hell was happening? She stood, too twitchy to stay still.

Outside the window, she spotted movement. Four armed men wearing black tactical gear climbed over the backyard fence.

Her stomach dropped as they advanced toward the house.

~

THE CORNER MARKET OFF BARN ROAD HAD FAR MORE customers than Zach would've preferred. Apparently, a snowstorm was approaching, and the locals wanted supplies.

The line crept forward. Two more customers and he'd finish fetching the goods.

Zach snorted. Here he was, on the run for his life, and he stood in a corner mart with a basket full of snacks, bread, and juice. On the way inside he'd checked for any tails, then he searched through the mart to make sure he never faced any of the video cameras.

None of the locals looked familiar either. Soft rock music from the eighties floated down to him from speakers overhead and he hummed along. He'd be fine for now.

As he got closer to the counter, he sidled up to the candy selection. And boy did this place have the good stuff. Lark had always wanted candy when he made a coffee run during their time in the hospital waiting room.

"Bring me an Almond Joy if they got it," she'd always say.

Zach thought that any candy bar stuffed with coconut and almonds tasted like shit, but Lark pumped her fist every time he managed to score one.

He spotted the Almond Joy candy bars on the bottom row and grinned.

She might still be pissed at him, but maybe he could score a point or two for effort.

A couple minutes later, the older woman in front of him shuffled up to the counter. She only had a loaf of bread in her hands, but she had quite the tale to tell the clerk about her grandson's first birthday.

Zach chuckled. Looked like Lark would have to wait a bit longer for that Almond Joy.

"You gotta be kidding me..." Lark backed up until she bumped into the counter behind her.

Those guys definitely weren't the neighbors bringing brownies and a warm welcome to the local hideout.

Two men continued toward the back door, while the others slipped around the side of the house.

They're blocking all the exit points.

She turned off the lights to the kitchen, then scrambled to check the drawers for weapons. With only the faint twilight to guide her, she found the search taxing. A single drawer offered some sizable meat cleavers, but as she palmed a rather sharp butcher's blade, she doubted she'd make much headway against multiple foes.

Zach had said this place was a safe house. That meant there had to be weapons somewhere in here.

So where would they keep them? Dad had peppered weapons in every nook and cranny in her childhood home. You couldn't fish out a mint from a candy bowl in the living room without uncovering some brass knuckles.

Lark scrambled out of the kitchen, checked the hall closet next to the front door, and found nothing but cobwebs. As she rushed into the bedroom, shutting the door behind her, she caught the heavy thud of someone slamming their shoulder against the heavy door.

Shitty. Shit. Shit.

At least the windows had bars. That would buy her some time before they figured out how to get inside.

She shoved the dresser in front of the bedroom door. Time to find some toys with bullets.

During her undergraduate studies, her dad might've thought she spent her spare time on campus studying and hanging out with her friends, but she'd joined the Marksmen Club instead.

And when Dad wasn't looking, Uncle Vincent slipped her gifts now and then. From a switchblade as a high school graduation gift to Aunt Gretchen offering her a selection of pepper spray.

"Knives are nice and all," Uncle Vincent had said, *"but you need a one-and-done deal."*

While she searched under the bed, the slams ceased. Only professionals would be able to get through those doors.

Finally, she scrambled to the closet and hit the mother lode. Right smack dab in the middle of the master closet lay an ancient steel-gray Browning gun safe.

The lock mechanism was mechanical with a dial. She turned the dial and prayed somebody had left it open.

Nope.

Well, it didn't hurt to try.

"Fine, fuck you too," she said.

Outside the bedroom door, she caught the thud of the back door hitting the floor. Damn, she didn't want to be caught alone in here.

Where the hell was Zach?

She should've asked for the code so she could open the safe.

Right on top of the dresser, she spotted the phone he'd let her borrow.

Of course the phone was charged. Ha. Good old Zach would've considered that. She turned on the phone and found one phone number in the address book: *The Red Hunter.*

She furiously typed out a message and hit send.

The tat stretched along her body, slithering from around her waist to extend from her neck to wrap around her leg.

"Behave," she said.

Light footsteps echoed outside the door. She clutched the butcher knife and pressed her back against the far wall.

If she had to stand her ground, she'd do it here.

Suddenly, the doorknob clicked as someone attempted to open the door. When the door didn't open, they tried to force their way inside. The dresser rocked back and forth until the door broke inward. Armed men stormed into the room.

Wide-eyed, she held her ground.

"Hands up!" the first man barked.

RIGHT OUTSIDE THE MART, ZACH'S PHONE BUZZED WITH an incoming message. Only three people had this number, and Cynthia or Kaden wouldn't text.

Cyn always wanted to hear his voice.

It was Lark.

His stride quickened as he pulled the phone from his pocket. A quick scan revealed a short message: *Hunters coming. Run.*

A rush of adrenaline propelled him to his car. Had she really told him to run? Not today. Not anymore.

Instead of sliding into the driver's seat, he jumped into

the back. From a duffel bag, he grabbed a Kevlar vest and rounds of ammunition. Sliding into his gear was second nature. Every movement he made was smooth and efficient.

Yet nothing could contain the rage edging into his senses. The fury surging into his racing heart.

He should've *never* left her alone.

The falling snow made the roads slippery, but Zach had driven through rougher terrain than this. His frantic pace through the neighborhood slowed once he reached the street. His breath quickened.

The hunters had to be waiting for him. But did they wait right outside of the house or inside?

He walked up to the house with an easy stride. Let them think he didn't know what was coming.

At the second step right outside the door, he paused. A new scent crossed his nose. The edges along the door appeared smashed in. He sucked in a deep breath.

Hunters had breached the house.

And if they'd touched her, they'd never know what hit them.

[5]

"Murdock, sweep the room," the man closest to Lark ordered the tallest one of the bunch. She couldn't make out many of his features under his helmet and goggles. Only that he had a well-cut beard speckled with black and white hair.

He was a veteran hunter. Those people could be deadly if she wasn't careful.

Two men waited in the living room with their guns pointed at the front door. The other two, Murdock and this asshole ordering everyone around, stared her down.

Murdock checked the closet. Finding it empty, he said, "Where's the wolf?"

"He's not here," Lark whispered.

"She's lying, Drake." Murdock loomed over her, flashing his gun as if she didn't know how they worked. "He's probably hiding in the attic."

Drake turned to the two hunters in the living room. "Quincy, monitor the door. Featherby, check the attic."

"I told you he's not here," Lark bit out.

"The outdoor sensors detected two people. One of them had a wolf's temp," Drake said.

So that's how they knew we were here. Why hadn't Zach known about the sensors?

Maybe because he wasn't a hunter anymore and the clans suspected he'd try a nearby hideout.

While Featherby checked the attic from the ladder in the hallway, Lark eyed her only path to escape: the front door.

She needed to buy time to figure out how to get out of this mess. "He was holding me prisoner, you know."

"Yeah, right," Drake drawled.

She pointed to her head dressing. "Do I look like I'm a threat to him? I'm a legacy from the Azzurro clan. He's trying to buy safe passage through us."

Murdock laughed. "Azzurro ain't shit no more. Even if you are a *legacy*, they don't have the power to help him." His grip clamped down on the back of her neck like a steel bracelet.

The snake curled inward on her back.

"You're hurting me!" She clawed at his gloved hand.

"McGinnis should be back soon. We'll use her as bait to make him come to us," Murdock said.

A comm on Drake's shoulder crackled, then a woman said, "Incoming. Our target has arrived. ETA thirty seconds. It's him."

"You heard that, boys," Drake drawled. "We finally got McGinnis this time."

Murdock dragged her out of the bedroom and down the hallway toward the living room. Once there, he shoved her to the couch. "Stay."

Murdock joined Drake and the other two as they took positions around the room behind furniture for cover.

Lark's heart jumped to her throat. Had her warning

meant nothing? Did Zach really think he could walk in here with semiautomatic weapons in play?

Murdock stooped not far from her right next to the front door. He clearly planned to strike Zach the moment the door opened.

Something glinted from the floor near the sofa. It was the shears Zach had left on the coffee table for the first-aid kit.

The front door lock clicked.

Lark reached until her fingertips brushed against the fallen shears. Once her hands wrapped around them, she took a deep breath, then lunged forward.

Time to play with sharp things.

She aimed for his face, but Murdock twisted to the side. The shears rammed into the hard surface of his helmet. Pain shot into her hand, eliciting a hiss from her clenched teeth.

Drake's comm blared. "We have lost visual. I repeat. We have lost—"

"Stupid bitch!" Murdock tried to hit her with his weapon's stock. In the midst of the chaos, the back door opened instead of the front. They turned in unison to see Zach storm into the house.

"What the hell?" Quincy grunted.

"About time!" Drake snapped. "Open fire!"

The roar of gunfire filled the room.

Murdock grasped Lark's arm and roughly shoved her toward the TV. She rolled over the ancient TV stand and collided with an end table and lamp.

Ugh. Now *everything* hurt.

From where she lay, all she caught was a blur of Zach, clad in all-black body armor, leaping across the room with his arm in front of his face. He roared and charged, throwing a fast roundhouse kick to Murdock's head. The blow connected and the hunter fell to the ground with a hard thud.

Suddenly, the snake came to life. It wrapped around her upper chest again and again until it stopped and *tightened.*

Bullets continued to fly. Many of them hit Zach, but he never paused, switching targets with precision.

The whole situation seemed surreal. Zach growled and snapped at them, his eyes golden and stormy as he tore at Drake and flung the man into the kitchen. The hunter crashed into the fridge before falling to the floor.

The other two hunters fell back and scrambled for a safer position. Zach jumped into the kitchen over the counter separating the dining room from the kitchen, breaking the overhead living room light.

Even with parts of the room bathed in darkness, she could hear Drake's grunts and screams.

"Armor-piercing rounds," Quincy shouted.

Featherby hurried to reload a new clip.

They took position near the kitchen and aimed in Zach's direction.

No, she thought.

The clenching grew tighter, forcing her to hold her breath. When she thought her ribs would crack from the pressure, the air burning in her lungs rushed out. Her fists released. Then her eyes opened, and the pain ebbed. With a sudden rush, her back spasmed and everyone around her was tossed into the air like cast-off toys. One hunter bounced off the dining room table and fell to the floor with a loud crunch.

Zach was the only one to rise. His eyes had darkened. His chest heaved with heavy breath as blood from his wounds dripped to the floor.

What have I done?

Lark glanced from the fallen men to the predator that stood before her.

No, what has he *done to them?*

She'd heard tales of the wolves' savagery, how once they smelled blood, they lost control and struck out at anyone. Would this wolf kill her too?

Lark shuddered. The man in front of her was no longer the one she'd fallen in love with.

~

A HUNGER FOR CARNAGE AND CHAOS RUSHED THROUGH Zach's veins as he stared her down.

Lark trembled before him, cradling her right shoulder. The man who'd touched her would *never* do it again.

The tide of emotions—rage and protectiveness—running through him was almost overwhelming. Before he'd become one, he had no idea how werewolves truly felt. How a simple fight could leave him feeling heady and hungry.

"Are you hurt?" He almost didn't recognize his own voice.

Who was in control now? The wolf or the man?

She took a wobbly step back.

He repeated the words again, but she didn't reply.

The fear in her eyes slapped him like a brisk mountain wind. He turned away from her and glanced down at his hands. A human being's hands. But they were covered in blood. He wiped them on his body armor. Little good that would do, though, since that was covered in blood too.

He shifted to the hunters and winced. A few hits had gotten through his vulnerable spots. During the fight, he'd only thought of his targets. Not the silver bullets they spewed.

Zach had to keep moving, so he checked the hunters. Quincy and Featherby were unconscious—they'd live another day. He recognized them from past hunter gatherings. At least he'd send them home to their families today.

But Drake and Murdock were another matter.

To keep him busy—and from falling over from the increasing pain in his sides—he gathered the weapons and ammunition.

When Lark didn't move, he tilted his head in her direction. She'd ambled over to the last working chair in the dining room and slumped into the seat.

What the hell had happened to her?

He hungered to draw her into his arms to check if she was well, but he'd only frighten her.

Something strange had gone down. One minute, Quincy and Featherby had planned to fill him with armor-piercing rounds, and in the next, she emitted a powerful force.

Not from her. *From the tattoo.*

There was also a tinge of electricity in the air. Just like the night when the woman in white had caused the explosion.

"We need to leave," he said, his voice less gruff. "Reinforcements will come if their lookout doesn't report a successful outcome. We got five minutes."

He caught her nod. She shuffled to the other side of the room.

"Do you know where my coat is?" he asked.

"It's got a lot of blood on it."

He sighed and fished a trench coat from the closet near the front door. She wouldn't be making any fashion statements, but it would keep her warm.

"This one doesn't have were-cooties on it." He extended the coat and waited.

Four long breaths later, she took the coat and put it on.

Zach grabbed a duffel bag from the bedroom closet and tossed the weapons inside. She was already out the door and heading to the car with the keys.

Damn, he must've really scared her.

She got in on the driver's side, turned on the headlights, and started up the car.

Would she leave him?

Probably.

But Lark stared at the sedan dashboard while he stowed the duffel bag in the back seat. She didn't head out until he settled into the passenger side and closed the door.

[6]

THE TWO AND A HALF HOURS SPENT DRIVING NORTH UP I-5 should've passed in a blur, but Lark couldn't shake what had happened.

Even with a bruise on her stomach bothering her, she tried to focus on driving, but the attack from a couple of hours ago kept playing on repeat through her head.

I have a damn snake tattoo and it just knocked out a bunch of people, she thought. *Let's add to that my former boyfriend showing up out of nowhere, and now he's a damn werewolf.*

What was next? Aliens coming out of the sea? Godzilla crawling out of Mt. Rainier? Hell, she wouldn't blink if that happened.

The gorilla—or should she say snake—in the room slid across her shoulders. She shivered, and Zach tilted his chin her way.

At this point, what good would it do for him to know about her problem? Any minute now, he could strike out at her just like he had those men.

And just when she thought she couldn't take the silence

anymore, her traitorous stomach grumbled so loud that Zach wouldn't need werewolf hearing to miss it.

"You hungry?" he asked.

She didn't look his way, focused on placing her hands on the proper places on the wheel.

"You never got a chance to eat," he added. He reached behind him and retrieved a white plastic bag from the back seat. "I grabbed some ramen, but we don't have a microwave, so I guess you'll have to settle for almond happiness?" He offered the bar of chocolate, and her resolve began to chip.

Damn him.

She gave him the evil eye. He knew her weaknesses too well.

"I don't want it," she mumbled.

Her stomach gurgled again as if on cue.

He chuckled, and she caught his widening grin. "You say no, but I don't think your stomach believes you."

She frowned and extended her hand for the food. "Fine. Give it to me... Please," she added softly.

He gave her not just one, but two Almond Joy bars. Damn him and his generous spirit.

She tried to rip open the wrapper, but she couldn't manage with one hand on the wheel, so she tore the plastic with her teeth. She'd been in a firefight not too long ago, so why bother being ladylike?

The first bite melted in her mouth, a perfect combination of coconut, almonds, and milk chocolate. Absolute. Bliss. She had no idea why so many of her friends hated the stuff.

"Who eats *coconut* in a candy bar?" one former classmate had said, while another annoyed friend told her that only a brainwashing cult would *poison* almonds with dark chocolate. She wanted to tell them they were referring to Mounds instead of Almond Joy, but why bother?

Fools, all of them.

Those poor people didn't know what they were missing. Hershey's was onto something when they called it Almond Joy, but she used the name Almond Orgasm instead.

Beside her, Zach turned on the radio, and old-school rap filled the car. With a frown, she switched the channel to a more mellow selection of soft rock.

Perfect.

"I can't do Doug E. Fresh during my culinary orgasm," she said with a mouthful of food.

Zach rolled his eyes, but she caught his amused expression.

For a moment, he felt like the old Zach. Just the two of them driving up I-5. Too bad the world was upside down right now.

By the time they passed Bellingham and approached the border to Canada, an uncomfortable silence bounced back and forth between them.

"Are you sure your...*friend* will let us through without passports?" she asked.

She finally glanced at him and caught his steady profile. He'd taken off the body armor, but his open coat didn't conceal his hole-laden T-shirt, or the blood peppered along his midsection.

"The Red clan always has a sentry on the border," he explained.

"Won't they be looking for you?"

"Yes, but you don't have a bounty on your head." He swallowed and winced. "Before we get there, I want you to drop me off. I'll cross into Canada on my own, and I'll meet you at The Hunting Grounds." He described what the sentry wore and how she should get into the correct border-crossing lane.

She eyed him with suspicion. How hurt was he?

"Tell them you're with the Azzurro clan," he added, "and your passcode is *Red Alpha Gamma Chi.*"

She nodded.

They were almost to the Ferndale exit, and he directed her to turn off. Halfway off the exit ramp, he told her to pull onto the shoulder.

Apprehension settled into her stomach.

"Are you sure about this?" As hard as she tried, she couldn't force herself to look at his face. Especially when he got out of the car and retrieved the duffel bag from the back seat.

She rolled down the passenger-side window in case he had additional instructions.

"Don't want you to have to worry about these." From her peripheral view, she saw him leaning against the door. "Don't stay out in the open for too long. The Red hunters will be looking for you in the Vancouver area."

Cars passed them.

Don't look at him, Lark.

Moving on alone was a good thing. She waited for the jubilation. Wasn't she about to be free from him again? Hadn't she told him she didn't need him?

That was before the attack, though. Before she'd learned she needed to seek out these "guardians."

A sliver of fear pulsed through her. She still had enemies searching for her. Why would she need guardians unless she needed protection against some bad shit?

Her fingers flexed against the steering wheel. Then she looked at him.

Damn, even beat up, he was still hot as hell, but he leaned to the left. How many of those bullets had hit him? Why did he have to play the hero all the time and not say anything?

Zach reached into his inner coat pocket and pulled out

another Almond Joy. A third one. Instead of handing it to her, he tossed it on the passenger seat. "You'll be fine, Lark. This *orgasm* should hold you over for a little while."

What a smart ass.

She snorted and slowly shook her head with amusement.

He lingered longer than she'd prefer but didn't say anything else. What could be said?

She opened her mouth to speak, but instead of asking about his health, she blurted, "See you on the other side, Z."

She forced herself to drive off.

The rest of the drive up I-5 to the border was bathed in quiet. At first, she tried a classic rock station, but when "If I Could Turn Back Time" by Cher came on, she turned it off. The last thing she needed was Cher reminding her about failed relationships.

She could imagine him hauling the duffel bag toward the border. He'd march for miles while healing from bullet wounds.

Ugh, why do you make me feel like such a fool? she thought.

At the next exit, she spewed a few curses and turned around. Yes, she was doing the right thing. No, she shouldn't change her mind about them.

But once she reached the Ferndale exit, she couldn't see anyone walking along the evening road or through the woods.

He was long gone.

She tried to call his cell, but a message told her that the phone's owner had turned the phone off. She couldn't reach him to tell him to come back.

Just like when he left the first time.

The moon hid behind thick clouds as Lark approached the border. Only the lights along the border crossing illuminated the lanes into Canada.

She spotted the sentry on the fourth lane. The man

wearing a red baseball cap had even left a red paw-print decal on his window. The line of cars this evening was long, especially for the sentry's line, but she eventually pulled up next to him.

As instructed, she gave the code, and the sentry inspected her car. No requests for identification. The whole experience was rather underwhelming—until she hit the outskirts of Vancouver.

I'm home again.

Boundary Bay loomed to the west outside the window. The fresh air from the Pacific should've filled her with calm, but she dreaded her next destination.

Twenty minutes later, she pulled into a parking garage in the trendy Granville neighborhood. This used to be her area. Her dad picked the perfect place near the intersection of Granville Street and West Broadway to open a pub. The area had plenty of popular restaurants and well-trafficked bars. Even the University of British Columbia campus was less than an hour away by bus.

She wasn't sure how long she sat in the car—at least long enough for her to have to turn the heat down and for her stomach to form fifty knots. The snake's head undulated on her right shoulder. Back and forth. Forth and back.

Let's do this, Lark, she thought. *It's time.*

She left the car and trudged down Granville Street. Nestled between a small private parking lot and a well-known gym, what was left of The Hunting Grounds was a boarded-up brick building. Scorch marks still lined the walls, and graffiti marked a few boards.

Seeing the unlit neon sign made her heart squeeze painfully. Two years ago, she'd stood here and met Zach for the first time. Has he been here since the fire eight months ago?

To distract herself, she searched for familiar faces, but no one waited in front of the building or nearby. Plenty of folks passed by—it was Saturday night, and even with the cold, the streets would be packed with folks going out to eat and party.

Foreigners on vacation walked by speaking languages she shouldn't understand—Mandarin, Russian, and Hindi—yet all of them blended in her head. All those conversations formed an English avalanche she couldn't block out.

Two women blathered about how lost they were, while a family from Ukraine couldn't wait to eat at the Cactus Club Cafe.

More weird shit. Was she losing her mind?

Unsure what to do, she shuffled toward the building and pressed her back against the steady wall. She scanned the streets. What would her guardians look like? Should she expect some huge guys dressed *Men in Black* style?

The big meetup had to happen soon. The tattoo squirmed up a storm on her shoulder. Did that mean anything?

A crowd of men and women, laughing and joking, turned the corner. Lark lifted the trench coat's hood over her head and stuffed her hands in her pockets—only to find something in the left pocket. It was heavy and metallic.

She fished out a set of military-grade spiked brass knuckles. Very nice. She almost whistled and noticed the crowd nearby. Nothing like flashing your weaponry to the public to get a free ticket to crazy-person-ville. What else would she find in a hunter's coat?

A hand tapped her shoulder. She jumped and glanced to her left to see a short Asian woman smiling up at her. Not that Lark was tall by any means at five foot five—which meant this woman had to be a couple inches shorter.

The woman adjusted her red glasses on her face, gave

Lark a nod, and said, "I was freezing my butt off waiting for you."

So, this was her *guardian*?

The bar-hoppers reached their destination, leaving Lark to gape at the woman. She noted the tiny woman's bright blue coat, black snow boots, and cheerful lime-green cap.

Was this a disguise, maybe?

"Sorry," Lark managed to say.

"I'm Janet, by the way. Born and raised in the area." Janet pointed down the street. "Brian had to go to the bathroom. Said something about not being able to hold it for much longer."

"Brian? Is that my other guardian?"

Janet nodded. "When did you get hurt?"

"It's a long story," Lark said with a short laugh. She had so many questions, but where should she start? "Umm, this is going to sound crazy, but do you have a *moving* tattoo too?"

Janet pursed her thin lips. "I got some sassy ink…but none of them move." She laughed as if they'd shared a joke. "I had this strange dream last night. I don't remember much, only that I had to come here tonight and wait for you."

"You saw *me* in your dream?"

"Very vividly. Weird, huh?"

"Whoa…that's deep." And creepy…

Janet's wide grin almost made Lark feel better. Almost.

The woman was about as tall as her aunt Gigi. But then again, nobody messed with Aunt Gigi. Short folks tended to be scrappy as hell.

They didn't have to wait long for someone else to show up. A lanky Indian man walked up to them with a casual wave.

"She's here!" Janet declared proudly to who had to be Brian.

Lark gave a weak smile. If these were her guardians, she

was screwed, but then again, maybe they were packing serious heat?

"Now that the team's all here, where should we go?" Janet asked.

"To be honest, I don't understand any of this. I more or less woke up with a weird tattoo and was told to meet you two here."

Brian stood on the corner with his arms crossed, and Lark tried not to find the situation ridiculous. Maybe Brian was a black belt in more than one martial art. Or he could be deadly like Uncle Vincent. That guy often had grenades in his back pocket.

"Do you live around here?" Janet asked.

"I—" Zach came to mind, but Lark shoved thoughts of him away. If she had Janet and Brian, she wouldn't have to endanger her friends. Or explain what happened.

"Should we go to your place, then?" Brian suggested.

She shook her head. Zach had warned her not to go home, but where else could they go? She didn't have money for a hotel room, and asking perfect strangers to foot the bill didn't feel right.

Might as well start with the basics first. Get as many answers out of them as possible, then leave them behind to keep them out of her mess. Lark directed them to where she'd parked the car. Brian walked ahead of them while Janet strolled beside her.

"So how long will this"—Lark gestured between the three of them—"guardianship last?"

"No idea," Janet replied.

"You don't have to help me. You probably have to work on Monday, right?"

Janet shrugged. "Don't worry about it. I can call work and explain everything."

And say what? she wondered.

"What do you do? Law enforcement?" Lark asked.

Ahead of them, Brian snorted.

"Oh no," Janet said. "I happen to be a licensed midwife specializing in natural birth."

Lark's stride slowed, and Janet kept pace with her. "Are you serious?"

"Yep, I've helped hundreds of babies enter the world."

Lark opened her mouth to ask Brian if he was an insurance adjuster—since that seemed like the next best occupation to keep her alive—but he paused, Janet right after him.

"Someone's following us," he murmured.

Janet looped her arm around Lark's. "Where?" she asked.

"They're maintaining a block's distance behind us," he said.

Could it be Zach?

"Was it a man?" Lark asked him.

"I can't tell." Brian picked up the pace. "They're tall and wearing a hood over their head. Whoever they are, they might not be alone, but there are too many people."

They crossed the street. Just two more blocks and they'd reach the parking garage.

Janet glanced over her shoulder. Lark was about to do the same, but Janet's grip on her tightened. "Don't. We need to blend in."

They were slowed down by a rowdy group leaving a restaurant. Lark could feel whoever was chasing them breathing down her neck. Brian was jogging now. Janet tugged her to follow.

What if Zach was following them? Should she run—or should she turn around and find him again?

A tall biker and his companion bumped into Janet, but the spry woman jerked back and seemingly gain two feet in two seconds.

"Watch where you're going," she griped.

"Sorry," the man blurted.

Janet urged them forward again, but not before Lark checked behind them. In the sea of faces, she didn't recognize any of them. Not good.

Had Zach run into trouble on the way?

Or was it even worse: he'd never planned to come at all?

They finally reached the garage.

"What floor?" Brian asked.

"Third. My car is in the far-left corner," Lark replied.

Brian led them to the nearest stairwell. Lark was grateful for the well-lit parking garage. If someone was after her, at least she'd see them coming. She stuffed her hand into her right pocket. If someone got too close, she'd introduce them to her brass-knuckled fist.

By the time they got up the first flight of steps, Lark's pace slowed and the ache on the back of her head returned. She stumbled up a step, and Janet caught her before she fell flat on her face.

She'd almost forgotten about her concussion. Good God, how was she supposed to make it up two more flights? Each step felt like someone was stabbing the back of her head with an ice pick, but Janet was having none of it. With the spunk of five Italian aunts, Janet helped Lark up the next flight.

"You can do it," Janet said. "One foot in front of the other."

At the bottom of the second floor, Brian remained behind. "Keep going. I'll slow them down and meet you at the east exit."

"Understood," Janet replied.

Is he crazy? Lark thought. They had no idea what they faced. Their pursuers could be armed.

"Take this." She fished the brass knuckles out of her pocket and tossed them to Brian. He caught the weapon but stared at them as if she'd handed him her bra.

Lark didn't have long to contemplate their next move. By the time Janet led her to the third floor, she could hardly put one foot in front of the other.

Keep moving, Lark.

They were almost to the car. She spotted the sedan. All they had to do was head up the incline to her car at the far end of the lot.

The snake tightened on her side. A warning like the attack from the hunters.

Something was coming. She glanced around. Nothing.

What could be chasing them? The serpent slid from her upper back down to the base of her spine. Her breath quickened. Would the snake strike out like it had before? She turned to Janet. Lark had barely met the woman, yet she might kill her.

A strange glow brightened the night to the west of the garage.

Her breath caught.

"Don't look back," Janet said.

Lark stumbled but caught her footing.

Suddenly, searing heat bathed her back. The force of an explosion sent her careening into a nearby car. Her chest hit the car hard, and with an *oof*, her breath was snatched from her lungs.

Beside her, Janet gasped and got to her feet. "You okay?"

The snake tattoo continued to slide faster and faster, making Lark's skin itch along the middle of her back. The strike was coming.

The urge to run strengthened until the ache at the back of her head grew in intensity.

"What the hell was that?" she mumbled.

Janet covered Lark the best she could with her smaller frame. "We're under attack."

Lark's father would've never cowered and waited to be

slaughtered. She forced herself to stand. There, step one done.

Janet tugged her again. "We're almost there."

Another explosion tore Janet away from Lark and sent her into the air. She watched in horror as Janet slammed into a nearby truck bed.

No one would survive that.

Lark stumbled backward—only to see a woman walk from between the cars. The stranger pulled back her black hood to reveal white-blonde hair shorn close to the scalp. The woman's attire was plain but expensive: dark gray trousers, a black wool coat, and leather boots. The alarm bells ringing in Lark's head intensified as the woman strode up to her. Lark widened her stance and clenched her fists. The tightening from the tattoo grew painful.

A talon on the tip of the woman's index finger caught Lark's gaze. Would the woman attack her with it?

Unable to believe her eyes, Lark watched the woman use the talon on her right hand to cut into her left. Once the blood from the deep wound spilled to the pavement, the blonde drew a strange design in blood on her wrist.

Lark took a step back, only for her mouth to drop open as fire glistened from Blondie's fingertips and danced up her arms.

What kind of crazy shit is this?

"You're coming with me," Blondie said.

"I think not," Lark breathed.

"I don't want to force you to go to Justine, but I will do what I must—"

The woman stopped as a dark form darted behind her. Blondie twisted. A massive, dark wolf jumped onto a nearby convertible then closed in fast.

More tightening near Lark's breastbone. She gasped for breath.

Blondie's confident smirk melted into a screech as the beast sent her hard to the concrete. The pair scrambled and tussled on the ground, but the woman never stood a chance. Burnt-orange flames flared from her hands, singeing the wolf's fur, but the wolf's powerful mouth clamped down on her shoulder and shook her hard.

Lark cowered from the blistering heat. She scrambled backward. "No," she whispered.

Could that wolf be Zach?

Unable to look away, she watched with rising horror as the wolf tore into Blondie. Then the screams began.

God help her, had her mother screamed the same way when werewolves attacked her? Had she pleaded for her life?

Lark checked her other pockets for a weapon, then the peculiar voice returned. The snake spoke again.

Strike him down, the thin and heady voice said to her. *Break his bones.*

Then the snake held still. Clenching. Holding. Preparing to hurt her enemies at her command.

But she never had a chance to answer the tat. Blondie went limp as a frigid breeze swept across the garage.

A faint car alarm buzzed nearby, but all Lark could do was look at the wolf staring at her. Its bright hazel eyes reflected an unnatural light and refused to blink. She could fall into them too easily. Her whole body froze and the snake released its hold.

Would the wolf attack her now?

The animal was enormous—its size double that of a man. It was hurt, though. Smoke rose from its flank, and patches of its fur had been burned away. Even though it was injured, it could overwhelm her with ease. Yet the wolf didn't move.

She swallowed deeply and looked closer. There was something familiar about those hazel eyes and the flecks of green within. But shouldn't those eyes be hypnotizing? Beautiful, yet cruel?

Moments passed, and the sirens of approaching police cars forced her to look away.

When she glanced up, the black wolf had disappeared. But past experience told her she had to be vigilant. She crawled toward the nearest car then used the door handle to support her while she stood.

Once she was upright, she surveyed the aftermath of the fight. Several cars had scratches and dents. The one beside her had shattered windows. And not far from her, blood pooled around a slain woman.

The blonde woman's fingers twitched.

Was she still alive? Lark took a few tentative steps closer. Bloody scratches covered the woman's hands. They were far too tiny to be claw wounds from a wolf, though.

Blondie drew a final wet breath, then she was still.

Checking her attacker's pockets would answer some of her questions, but Lark needed to find Janet and Brian. She squeezed her eyes shut and willed herself to move.

Damn it all to hell, no more than a half-hour into finding them, she'd gotten them killed.

It didn't seem fair.

Nothing is fair in life, her heart reminded her.

As quickly as she could, while watching out for the wolf, she returned to the royal-blue truck to find Janet. When she reached the end of the truck, she prepared herself for what she'd find, but when she peered into the back, it was empty.

"Janet…" she whispered.

Had Janet dematerialized when she'd died?

Anything crazy was possible at this point.

Lark searched around the car and discovered Janet's boot on the other side. Along with a faint trail of blood. Her heartbeat quickened as she circled the Ford Explorer next to the truck.

Please let her be alive.

At the end of the blood trail, Lark found Janet propped up by the concrete wall. She was breathing.

"Oh my God. You're alive." Lark pressed her hand against Janet's forehead. "You're burning up. Let me get the car. We'll get you to the hospital."

Lark hurried to the sedan while fishing the key from her pocket. Once she reached the driver's side, she came to a hard stop when she saw a man dressing on the other side.

Zach slid into a black T-shirt. "Took you long enough to get here."

[7]

"Long enough. Are you kidding me?" Lark said.

Zach shook his head while he slipped on his military-grade boots.

"Sooner or later you were going to see what I've become." His jaw tightened. "I wish I had time to prepare you, but we ran into trouble back there."

"Trouble?" Was he serious? "There's a dead woman back there."

"She's not human."

"Well, whatever she was, she doesn't have a pulse anymore."

He folded his arms. "She's trailed you since you left the pub, and if she planned to chat, she wouldn't have brought her little campfire along."

Her open mouth snapped shut.

Should she believe him?

Zach had never lied to her—other than the standard stuff most couples kept from each other. Morning breath, bad hair days, and all.

But what bothered her most was if that woman had

71

planned to meet her with good intentions, why did Blondie attack Lark's guardians?

Because that bitch meant to harm you if you hadn't cooperated.

Her hands formed fists, and she forced herself to move while Zach leaned against the driver's-side door.

"Move." She glanced at his face. Burns marred his cheeks and neck. A bullet hole here and there remained, but bit by bit, the smudged skin peeled away to reveal blemish-free skin underneath.

He was a werewolf, after all.

"Why?"

She refused to look at him again. If she took in the lines of pain in his brow or his growing frown, she'd ask him if the burns hurt or if he needed help. An ache formed in her heart, and she counted to three to push the feeling away.

She forced herself to sigh. "Please move. I need to get Janet to the hospital and find Brian."

"That woman planned to apprehend you, Lark."

"I know," she bit out.

"Running away from an unseen enemy isn't wise. We need to figure out who hired her. She mentioned someone named Justine."

"Later." She stopped herself from shoving him away. "Will you please move?"

Zach rolled his eyes and jerked his head to behind her.

"What?" she grumbled.

He grabbed her by the shoulder and twisted her around.

Lark's mouth dropped when she saw Janet, missing a boot, and Brian standing behind the short woman.

"What happened to you two?" She approached them. "Are you okay?"

The horrible gash on the side of Janet's head had vanished. Lark forced herself to swallow. More magic?

Brian appeared worse for wear. His coat was ripped in a few places, and soot darkened his pants. Bloodstains covered his flannel shirt lapel.

Janet peered around Lark to check out Zach. "You know him?"

"Yeah, I know him, but he's dangerous," Lark said.

Janet surged forward, growled, and pushed Lark behind her. The former hunter didn't even flinch.

This couldn't be happening. She stepped away from Janet and glanced between the three of them.

"You didn't know, did you?" Zach asked Lark with a smirk.

What had she missed this time?

"They're werewolves," he said.

No fucking way.

Her gaze flicked to Janet, who shrugged, while Brian refused to look at Zach's nonchalant expression.

"Did either of you plan to tell me?" she asked her guardians.

"We thought you knew," Brian said. "You're the one that summoned us—"

"And I don't even know how I did that either." Lark gave a sad laugh. That chuckle didn't give her the clarity she'd wanted. "This isn't going to work."

"Did we do something wrong?" Brian glanced at Janet.

"Just go walk the perimeter for a bit," Zach told them. "I'll talk to her."

Janet shifted to move, but Brian stood his ground. "Who are you to tell me what to do?" he asked. "To tell *us* what to do?"

Zach simply crossed his arms, but Janet tapped his shoulder.

"I think she'll be okay with him," Janet said. "We won't

go far away. Let's see if we can find any identification on that woman who attacked us."

Once the pair left, Lark took in the concrete. The cracks in the floor didn't have any answers. Too much had taken place in the last couple of hours. Any minute now, the remains of her overwhelmed gray matter would be oozing out of her ears onto the concrete.

Those damn werewolves lurked around every corner.

EVERY INCH OF ZACH'S BODY ACHED AS THEY DROVE through town. They were about half a mile away from the garage and police vehicles.

In the back seat, Janet and Brian were examining something, while Lark faced away from him in the passenger seat.

He blinked and almost cursed. Even *blinking* was a bad idea.

His arms and legs had spewed out the silver bullets not too long ago, but fragments still remained and scratched away at his insides like shattered glass.

Lark glanced at him, and he released the breath he held. He refused to show her his suffering.

Give her time, he reminded himself.

She'd always needed time to adjust to new circumstances.

But how much time did he have before she walked away for good? She had witnessed what Kaden had called Zach's *true form.*

There was no going back.

He had a lot of things to say to her: was she beyond pissed? Could they talk about it later?

So many questions weighed on him, but now wasn't the time to broach them. *Safety first.* Questions later.

"You got her phone?" Zach asked his new cohorts in the back seat.

"Yeah," Brian replied.

"How did you get into it?" Lark asked, not bothering to look away from the window. Yep, she was that mad at him.

"Umm, we pressed her finger to the home button enough times to change the password," Brian whispered.

Zach nodded. They'd done what they had to do.

Lark slowly shook her head.

"Find out anything about her so far?" Zach asked.

Brian twisted the phone around in his hand. "This is a top-of-the-line model. Which means our attacker is loaded or her employer pays well."

"Oh, I could tell you all the specs," Zach said, "but I want to know more specifically if you can identify her. Name. Address. Contacts?"

"Already on it. I work...worked as a risk-assessment analyst for a bank. She doesn't have any identifying information on the phone's account."

"It's a burner phone?" Zach asked.

"Not exactly. She's not logged into any social media accounts, but she was corresponding with two people through text messages." Brian's fingers swept over the screen while Janet leaned in to watch.

"Let me see," she whispered.

Zach took them in. Janet and Brian were what werewolf packs called rogues—werewolves without a pack. They didn't smell *connected*, like Kaden's people. Each of the werewolves in Kaden's pack had a faint scent that linked them—almost as if they used the same soap. These wolves had no such signature. Janet smelled liked she'd doused herself in essential oils, and Brian smelled like he'd walked out of a corporate environment with endless days of pencil pushing.

Neither of them had probably seen a day of combat. But

the spunk the pair had shown protecting Lark was admirable. Zach glanced at Lark, wondering what other secrets the tattoo held. At this rate, would he be alive to learn about them?

Their path away from the garage led them to the coast. He wasn't sure where to go. He had too many enemies here, and it would take just one sentry or camera to spot him and they'd have the Red hunting clan breathing down their necks.

He settled for northward out of Vancouver. The mountains would hide them for now.

Brian piped up from the back seat. "Apparently, the woman who attacked us was named Phoebe—"

"How suburban…" Janet said.

Brian frowned at her. "Phoebe was under orders from someone named Justine to find Lark and bring her to the train station tonight."

"And Phoebe failed," Zach said as a wave of anger touched him.

"She was also in touch with another party. A woman named Z. She offered a higher sum than Justine's offer for Phoebe to bring Lark to the Painted Coven so they could *contain* the new owner of the serpent."

"The Painted Coven," Lark whispered as she glanced in the rearview mirror. Now they had her attention. "Have either of you heard of them?"

Her guardians both shook their heads.

"Anything else in the messages?" Zach asked.

"Not much," Brian replied. "Just the terms. Phoebe mentioned it wouldn't take her long to deliver Lark to them since it would be a one-hour drive to their location…" He hummed as he read. "They told Phoebe to take the ten a.m. ferry from Hummingbird Bay—which means their rendezvous point would've been Bowen Island."

"It's not far from us. We should try to catch the next ferry," Lark said.

"Are you sure you want to go there?" Zach asked. "They hired an assassin—with peculiar powers, no doubt—to find you. She'd planned to auction you off the party that offered her the most money."

"I need answers," she said.

[8]

On their journey north through the night along I-5, Zach's gaze jumped from one passing car to another. Someone with strange powers had attacked Lark—which meant there could be more enemies tracking them.

To distract him from his darkening thoughts, he focused on the next morning. They'd reached the Hummingbird Ferry parking lot and decided to wait until the morning to set out.

Lark curled up on her side, still facing away from him, while the wolves in the back seat fell asleep, leaving Zach on guard duty.

He didn't mind. His insides were still stitching back together, and he wanted to use the time to search Phoebe's phone for any additional information he could uncover.

A half-hour later, he gave up. Brian had been thorough; Zach had to give the man that much credit. While the others slept away, he dug out his own phone. Through a VPN to protect his activities, he checked his email and found none. No messages, either. A year ago, his box would've been full of hunter business. Contract requests, freelancer referrals, and the like.

Now he had nothing.

At least he still had photos. He had hundreds of them in his photo app online. He browsed through them to find those he'd believed were his friends. Hunters hanging out at backyard cookouts after a long mission. Axe-throwing contests out at Glen's farm; the Red hunting clan's winter barbecue in Old Bart's backyard. Now that made him smile. All his old friends gathered together in the dead of winter with beer, burgers, and brats sizzling on a grill. What he wouldn't give for one gathering. One more legendary drinking contest.

All of that was gone now.

Before he had a bounty on his head, he'd checked in with his younger brother once in a while. Not that Ty wanted to hear from him. After Cyn fell ill, Ty disappeared. A part of Zach understood. Who'd want to witness their loved one's suffering?

But family was family.

He wished he call Ty to check on him, but after Cynthia became a werewolf, Ty had attacked her. Their little brother had chosen the hunters over them. The very thought that Ty didn't love them anymore left him uneasy.

Now he had no clan. No little brother. Just an open road and the unknown.

MORNING ARRIVED, AND WITH THE RISING OF THE SUN, the group grabbed some food then boarded the ferry to their final destination: Bowen Island.

As the waves broke against the ship, questions bombarded Zach: what would they find on the island?

Would he face adversaries as dangerous as the strange woman they'd encountered in the parking garage?

The breeze off the bay carried an array of scents across his nose. The wolf within yearned to roam the familiar forest with new eyes, but such a trip wasn't meant to be.

Only a fool headed to one of the Red hunting clan's training grounds, yet here he was. Was it a coincidence that was where Phoebe would've taken Lark? Was this all an elaborate plan to bait him?

He glanced at Lark. She appeared closed in, her arms folded. The gauze wrapped around her head was dirty and torn.

Janet sat next to her, while Brian performed guard duty several paces away.

To occupy his mind, Zach fetched a first-aid kit from the ship's steward. He strolled up to Lark, preparing himself for her refusal. The stubborn Lark he knew wouldn't say yes.

"Want me to change your dressing?" he offered.

She didn't even glance up at him. "I'm fine."

Janet looked from him to her. A grin touched her lips, and she extended her hand for the kit without a word. Begrudgingly, he handed Janet the kit and took his spot against the railing.

While he took in the coast, Janet retrieved materials from the box and cleaned the gash on the back of Lark's head.

A wave of jealousy touched him, and he didn't bother pushing the feeling aside. He should be the one healing her, caring for her, but she needed her space from him, and he should respect that.

No matter how much it bothered him.

Eventually, the ferry reached the island. Zach scanned their surroundings. To the east, the Cypress mountains and the mainland loomed. The island's tall pines and serene views greeted him. From what he remembered, the island's hilly forest terrain might present challenges for Lark, but he hungered to explore the forest around Mt. Gardner with his heightened perspective.

They disembarked and Lark chose to sit in the back seat, forcing Brian to join Zach in the front.

As they drove out of Snug Cove along Grafton Road, Brian broke the silence. "You're uneasy, friend." His words were barely a whisper. Words meant for only a wolf to hear.

Zach sighed and rolled down the window a bit. "That obvious, huh?" he replied just as quietly.

"If you weren't acting as a sentry, I'd say you're as antsy as a pup spotting its first fight."

Zach chuckled. He guessed he was a pup in a way.

Brian tilted his head a bit. "She might not get a warm welcome with this so-called Painted Coven."

"No, she might not, and we got other problems."

Brian nodded. "What other problems?"

"The Red hunting clan has a bounty on my head."

Brian snorted. "You and every other werewolf."

"Most bounties aren't over one hundred thousand dollars."

"What did you do?" Brian's smile deepened. He seemed impressed. He looked out the window to the two-lane road and the tranquility of pine, elm, and ferns. "Do they have a presence on the island?"

"Unfortunately, they have a training facility on the southern side."

Brian visibly swallowed. "Did they see us leave the pier?"

"I didn't spot any lookouts today, but usually we—*they* don't bother guarding locations with heavy hunting clan activity."

Brian nodded, appearing relieved. Had he caught Zach's slip-up? A year ago, Zach would've been the hunter, herding men and women like them into dark corners for slaughter. A part of him knew men and women like Brian and Janet existed—the werewolves that hid among the humans and hunted alone—but too many other rogues and power-hungry packs had dirtied the pool.

And now the hunting clans killed any wolves without mercy.

He glanced at Lark in the rearview mirror. He caught her light snoring. The sleep should do her some good.

His fingers tingled from where he'd touched her. Maybe he could try to heal her again later.

"How long has it been since you've been here?" Brian asked.

That was a loaded question, but Zach was grateful Brian hadn't gotten to the point. They had far too many other things to worry about instead of his hunter past.

"At least a couple years."

Brian gave him a side glance. "How long have you been running alone?"

"Feels like forever, but it's not." Zach kept his voice steady. "I could've joined the Windham pack, but I had too many hunters breathing down my neck to bring them trouble."

"The Windhams? I've heard of them. Didn't they have a run-in with the Cerulean clan recently?"

"Them and plenty of others."

"The hunters are the reason why I haven't found a pack." Brian lowered his voice. "The only good hunter is a *dead* hunter, I say."

Zach flexed his fingers on the steering wheel. "Not all hunters are bad—just like not all werewolves have bad intentions. You and Janet have done well for yourselves."

Brian opened his mouth to say more, but they approached the street mentioned in Phoebe's text messages: Mt. Gardner Road.

"You been down this way before?" Brian asked.

"This is new to me. I say we find a place to park and scout out the area for danger," Zach said. "Let her rest with Janet."

Brian nodded.

After two miles heading northeastward up the road, they pulled over and ventured into the woods. Zach glanced over his shoulder to the vehicle hidden among the trees. Instead of waiting inside the car, Janet had decided to do her sentry duties right outside the driver's-side door.

Pleased Lark wouldn't be in danger for a little while, he took point and headed northward, with Brian right behind him. He broke out into a light run, searching around for any paths or signs of humans.

Or hunters.

The Red hunting clan tended to stick to the lower half of the seven-mile-long island. They performed exercises inside the Fairy Fen Nature Reserve and rarely crossed Mt. Gardner to the witches' location in the north.

Many of the cabins and beach houses along the island's northern coast boasted scenic views and insane price tags. Old Bart had owned a place in Snug Cove, so he'd passed the property to the clan. Just traipsing around this island brought back memories of spending summers here with other hunters.

The thick birch and pine trees opened up to a field and a hill. Zach hurried upward, with Brian keeping pace. He wore a pair of running sneakers—not the best shoes for this terrain, but they couldn't take care of that problem for now.

At the top of the hill, a new scent emerged from the foliage. It was strangely coppery, like blood.

"Do you smell that?" Brian murmured.

The harsh crunch of dry leaves underfoot made Zach turn to see two women standing behind them.

Brian growled low in his chest.

They hadn't heard them approach. Not good at all.

The one to the far left was as tall as Zach, but far thinner, with shoulder-length strawberry-blonde hair and pale skin. She wore a black winter coat, jeans, and boots. The stout, dark-skinned woman beside her wore the same. The shorter woman glared at Zach and Brian, waiting for either of them to make their move. Her cheeks were rounded and forehead high. Zach had met hunters from Somalia who had similar features.

"These grounds are not for you," the tall woman said.

"This doesn't look like private property to me, friend," he replied, keeping his voice steady. Zach rested his right hand close to his side in case he needed to withdraw his P320 from the holster strapped to his torso.

The tall woman smiled. "We're not your friends. Phoebe should've delivered her to us—not you."

Now that Brian made twitch.

"Delivered her? Is Lark a package?" Zach returned the smile.

"The wolf doesn't understand, Yolande," the shorter woman said. "We won't be able to contain her if she waltzes in—"

"Shut up, Jamilah," Yolande hissed. Her hand rose when Jamilah took a step forward.

Zach gaze flicked between them. Every muscle in his legs tightened and his senses went into overdrive. In two steps, he could tackle them.

He shouldn't have left Lark alone.

"If you hurt her—" he started.

The women laughed.

"Calm yourself, Wolf." Jamilah took a step to his right then drew the sharp point of a pocketknife across her index finger. Blood pooled on the digit. Using the bloody finger, she drew three symbols on the palm of her other hand.

What was she doing?

Zach prepared to move, but before he could take one step forward, Janet and Lark materialized in front of them and fell to the ground.

The two women glanced around as if they'd been sitting in the car, and then looked up.

Zach rushed in front of Lark.

"What the hell just happened?" Lark whispered.

"I don't know," Zach replied. "But I don't like this."

Yolande's hard gaze softened. "You need to come with us," she said to Lark. Then to everyone else, "All of you."

Zach shook his head slowly.

"I don't often ask politely," Yolande said with a chuckle.

Janet glanced at Zach, and he nodded.

They needed answers, but Zach knew one thing was for certain: they wouldn't like what they learned.

[9]

LARK WASN'T SURE WHAT TO EXPECT, BUT AS SHE WALKED down the foot path off Mt. Gardner Road toward a clearing at the end, she was surprised to see a huge, beautiful stone courtyard leading to the backyards of three homes.

To her left, partially obscured by pine trees, sat a two-story light blue house with white shutters. In the middle, the largest home of the three boasted two levels and grand arched windows. The dark green siding was weathered, yet well preserved. It was the third house to the right that offered a bright set of colors: a vibrant crimson two-story home with a steeple on its roof. A set of elaborate decks made of cedar planks connected the homes' backyards and led to a small greenhouse to the far right and a storage shed to the far left. A wondrous breeze from the ocean whistled between the buildings and kissed her face. Beyond the houses, another island and mountains came into view. The houses had to be reach next to the shoreline.

Several figures waited for them on the back porch of the largest home. Even from the edge of the tree line where Lark

87

stood, many of their faces appeared blank and unwelcoming —but one in particular tugged her forward.

Beside her, Zach kept up with her quickening pace.

One of the figures stood taller than the others. Lark had seen that narrow face before. A mournful quiver filled her chest. She'd seen that same narrow nose and full lips.

On her mother.

The olive-skinned woman stepped away from the others and descended the porch steps. Her brown eyes widened as Lark drew closer. Now that Lark could see her fully, her gaze soaked in everything. This woman wasn't her mother—could she be a relative? She had her mother's light chestnut hair, but her eyebrows were far too thick, and her long arms clung to her sides.

Mama always stretched out her hand for Lark to take it.

Soon they stood before the welcoming party. Yolande and Jamilah walked around them to wait off to the side.

Did they believe Lark would attack?

Another woman, this one older than the first, with deep-set light blue eyes and short blonde hair, strode up to the olive-skinned one and touched her shoulder. "I know you're anxious to see her, but we need..."

The tall woman nodded. "I know."

"Do you know me?" Lark asked. "You look familiar."

"I'm your aunt Iluminada," the woman whispered, her dark brown eyes bright with joy.

"My aunt?" Lark couldn't contain the hollow feeling in her chest. All this time she'd been told her mother was an orphan, and yet here was her aunt. "I thought—"

"You have many questions," the blonde woman said, "and they should be answered out of the cold." She gestured toward the house. "Please come inside, where you can warm up so we can welcome you to the Mountain Haven House."

"O-of course," Lark stammered.

She headed up the stairs, and her aunt immediately drew her arm around her shoulders. "What happened to you?" She glanced at the bandage around Lark's head.

"I was in an accident at my job—it's a long story."

"I'm sure," Iluminada said. "Oh, *mi hija*, I'm so glad you found us."

Lark's heart jumped. Her mom used to call her that when she was a little girl. *My daughter.* No one had addressed her that way since Mom had died. How come she'd never met Iluminada before? What other secrets had her mother kept?

They strode through the back door into a large mudroom. Coats and shoes from large to small filled cubbies. Did children live here too?

They discarded their coats in the mudroom, and Yolande and Jamilah brought up the rear as they filed down a long hallway to a great room.

Lark's eyes widened. A beautiful Persian cat darted across gleaming pine floors. Luxury shone from the great paintings on the wall to the finely polished rustic furniture.

But as they settled onto couches, Lark noticed something else. A lack of personal items. No family pictures. Lark had yet to enter a family member's home where a child's drawing didn't adorn a wall or toys weren't cast aside in a corner.

Cold and *institutional* would be better words to describe what she'd seen so far. At the far end of the room, bookcases filled one side to the other. She couldn't see the titles, but none of the books appeared new.

The women stared at her, drawing her attention back to them. Janet sat next to Lark, while Brian and Zach chose to stand behind them. When she glanced at Zach, she couldn't read his stony facial expression. The only thing on him that moved was his eyes. They jumped from each person in the room periodically as if he was assessing them.

Should she be doing the same?

From a chair to her left, her aunt grasped her hand. "Do you need medicine? You look pained."

"She'll be fine once she warms up," the older woman said.

"Zenobia…" Iluminada said.

"Give her space." Zenobia leaned forward with a polite smile as Jamilah strode into the room with tea service on a tray. The poor cat had to jump out her way. She stiffly placed the cups before Lark, Iluminada, and Zenobia.

"Hey…" Why not Janet too?

With a curtness even Lark could detect, Jamilah hurried to pour a cinnamon-scented tea into the cups.

Iluminada winked at Lark. "You won't have to be a maid forever, Jamilah. At least pretend you don't mind."

Jamilah's cheek twitched with irritation.

"Jamilah is one of our protectors," Iluminada explained. "You would call them guards, but we refer to them as enforcers."

Lark glanced between the women. Her father had always taught her to read between the lines whenever possible. So far, this place made no sense. Was this place a cult of some kind? The dark garb didn't give off free-love vibes. A strict hierarchy existed between them.

As soon as Jamilah retreated with the tray to the kitchen, Lark reached for her cup, but Janet snatched her wrist.

"What—"

Janet picked up the cup, sniffed the drink, then took a sip. "It's fine."

Zenobia and Iluminada shared an amused expression.

"Why would they poison us?" Lark whispered to Janet.

"I don't know these people." Janet stared hard at Zenobia. "Trust should be earned."

Zenobia's pale face stretched out to a wide smile. "As it

should be." Her small hands grasped her tea, and she took a long drink.

Lark took the cup from Janet and sipped. The cinnamon tea was flavorful. "I'm not sure where to begin, but I guess simplicity works best." She drew a deep breath. "Who are you people? How did you know my mother?"

Iluminada opened her mouth to speak, but a glance from Zenobia silenced her.

"We are blood witches, Lark." Zenobia said as the cat leapt into her lap. "Just like your mother."

Lark felt her jaw slacken. "Witches? You're kidding, right?" she replied.

Zenobia slowly shook her head.

"We've been around for many centuries," Zenobia said, "practicing what you'd call magic using our greatest gift, the very blood that flows through our veins."

"And the tattoo?" Lark asked.

"That's all part of it," Zenobia explained. "This began with noble families in Europe. When a particular talent—like clairvoyance—was identified in girls, the families fostered the ability in secret. Over time, we determined that our powers could be improved and even heightened through the study of blood magic."

A familiar ache gathered at the back of Lark's head. The pain sparked movement from the serpent. This was all too much for her to take in.

Zach touched her shoulder and gently gripped it.

Zenobia scratched the cat's head and continued. "Your mother, Lupita, came from this coven, but twenty-five years ago, she left us for a new life on the outside."

Lark's brow knitted. From what her father had told her, her mother had told him she grew up in an orphanage, then, when she got old enough, she lived on her own on the streets.

So why the lies?

Something bad must've gone down here. Lark hungered to know more, but now wasn't the time to push too hard for the answers.

"Our gifts exposed us to a world beyond ours," Zenobia said, her voice growing quieter. "A place filled with demons and dark creatures that wanted into this plane of existence." The weight of her words pressed into Lark.

"I wish I could say our cause is noble, but we cursed ourselves," Iluminada added. "Hundreds of years ago, a blood coven tried to contact demons for divination, and during the ritual, demons possessed them and killed many innocent people."

"And the tattoos?" Lark asked. "Where did they come from?"

Iluminada's gaze flicked to Zenobia, who gave a faint nod. "One coven in particular, the Horned Owl Coven, was forced to make the ultimate sacrifice when a blood demon escaped its prison. It possessed a witch and she massacred an entire village in a remote region in Spain." Iluminada swallowed deeply. "One of their elders drew a great glyph, a spell to trade her lifeblood to trap the demon in her skin."

The serpent slid on Lark's back as if acknowledging the past events.

Iluminada continued. "When the serpent appeared on the witch's skin, the other witches rejoiced and used the same technique to capture the other demons…but there was a price."

"A bargain we *never* should've made," Zenobia whispered.

"The tattoos grant the wielders the ability to cast spells without spilling blood, but the blood demons under their skin feed on suffering and misery," Iluminada said. "Over the years, those painted witches have killed far too many innocent souls. Like the serpent you now possess."

Lark realized she was holding her breath and exhaled.

She could perform magic. Like the way she'd attacked those hunters. "So there's more tattoos out there."

Zenobia drew back the sleeve of her black tunic to reveal the tip of tentacle tattoo. The ink in her skin was dark pink with splashes of vermillion. The gray and white cat hissed peculiar sight—only to have Zenobia shush at it. Lark peered closer, only to shudder as the tentacle shrank back to hide under Zenobia's sleeve.

What in the fuck was that tentacle attached to?

"The gifts they grant can be beneficial in the right hands," Zenobia said with a raw intensity, "but in the wrong ones, they bring death."

"Death follows everyone." Zach's deep voice echoed through the room.

The silence after Zach spoke grew heavy until Lark ended it.

"Do all the demons take the form of an animal?" she asked.

"Yes, as far as I know," Zenobia replied. "As to why? We may never *want* to know the reason."

Lark emptied her teacup. Her aunt stood and poured another cup. Lark murmured her thanks.

"So if only blood witches can have this thing, that means I'm a witch, too," Lark said. Her head turned to cotton at the implications. "Does that mean I'm *possessed* right now?"

Zenobia frowned. "A blood demon didn't possess you. Another blood witch *granted* it to you." She paused and stroked the cat as if considering her words. "The previous owner of the tattoo is Folake Adesina. We haven't seen her in a very long time."

Annoyance flashed across Iluminada's features, but she hid it quickly.

Lark spoke the woman's name, and the unfamiliar vowels

rolled across her lips. "I have a feeling Folake won't be invited to visit the coven anytime soon."

"Like I said before," Zenobia said, "death follows the tattoos, and the body count following Folake was far too high. She relished the power her demon gave her, but I guess since you have it now, she finally decided to leave that life behind…and give it to you. Now you have her *burden*."

"Give it to me?" Lark barked. "You mean more like she forced it upon me."

Zenobia shrugged. "The tattoo can't be given to just anyone. Only a blood witch and only a woman who is what we call a *kindred spirit*. No one knows why those godforsaken creatures are so picky."

Lark nodded and rubbed the back of her neck. The subtle ache from her concussion hadn't gone away. "I have so many questions. I mean, how come I can understand a bunch of foreign languages now?"

Iluminada reached for Lark's hand and squeezed it. "I'm sure you have many questions, but there's time to answer them—after you've had some rest. We have time enough to get to know each other now."

Zenobia flicked her fingers, and Yolande stepped up to her. "Take Lark to the Lake House and make sure she's comfortable."

Yolande nodded.

They stood and filed out of the room the same way they'd come in. On the way out, Zach said, "You all are hiding something. Care to tell me now that your boss isn't present?"

Yolande quirked a brow but didn't speak as they strode across the courtyard to the house past the second one.

Zach continued. "The blood witch who tried to take Lark had orders from someone named Justine. Who is that?"

The witch paused, and Lark caught the pursing of her lips. "She is the devil himself under the guise of an angel."

[10]

EVERY FOE THAT ZACH HAD FACED HAD ALWAYS HINTED at the hand they would play during a game of chance. That gave him time to anticipate and react versus waiting for the blows as they came.

These mysterious women had given him more questions than answers. As a district manager who'd often had to make important decisions for the Red hunting clan, he found these women far more intriguing than any foe he'd encountered before.

Another peculiarity amused him as well. All the witches carried the same herbal scent he'd detected on Lark.

She was truly among her people.

As they walked into the light blue house next door, Zach surveyed their surroundings. This house had a swing on the back porch as well as a child's bicycle leaning against the side of the house.

Yolande led them inside, not saying a word or discarding her coat. She made the wolf within him uneasy. She walked as if she had military training, and he wouldn't bet against her having weapons underneath her coat.

Earlier she had revealed that they should fear Justine, yet what scared Zach the most was the blood demons. All his life, his parents had prepared him to hunt and kill were-wolves. Not once had he overheard them or the clan's sage mention such creatures. Which meant he was on his own at this point.

Yolande gestured around the large kitchen. "We call this home the Lake House. You're free to use this space and eat any of the food you find in the refrigerator. We weren't prepared for guests, as you can imagine," she said to Lark, "but you'll manage."

"Thank you." Lark appeared rooted to a spot near the door.

Zach had already reached the other side of the room. He'd counted multiple exits and entryways. The doors had nothing more than simple locks. The windows, covered in shutters, weren't reinforced with shatterproof glass like the ones he'd spotted in the previous house.

A glance into the living room confirmed his suspicions. Someone had left coloring books, crayons, and a pair of scis-sors in the middle of the floor. Children's drawings were taped to the walls in the living room. Whoever lived here had left in a hurry. The coat hooks next to the front door were empty. He inhaled, drawing in the scent of hot chocolate—only the hot chocolate had been left on a nearby coffee table. Right next to it sat a half-eaten cookie. He couldn't discern the ages of the children, only that they had been here recently.

"While you're our guest, we expect you to stay in the house." A smile slowly stretched across Yolande's lips. "But if you decide to leave, you don't have to tell anyone you're going."

Lark squared her shoulders. "My mother taught me to be polite. I'll let you know if I decide to leave."

Yolande turned to the werewolves. "Follow me. You'll be staying outside."

Janet shifted as if to follow Yolande, but Lark stopped her. "Excuse me?"

"Animals aren't welcome to stay in here," Yolande explained. "They can sleep in the cellar."

Lark gave a short laugh. "These people are my *friends*."

Zach crossed his arms and waited. He didn't detect malice in Yolande's stance, only amusement in the slight quirk of her grin.

"So be it," she said. "But please understand that so far we have treated them with courtesy, but werewolves usually don't *want* to be here."

"Why?" Lark asked.

"You'll understand soon enough. We have our ways, and you need to learn how to respect them. You are a blood witch, after all." With that, Yolande backed out of the room and left.

The moment she left, Janet said, "What a bitch."

"Pretty much," Lark replied.

Zach crossed the room and peered out of the back window. As he'd expected, Yolande and Jamilah stood guard on the other side of the clearing. With the curtains open, they could see into the house.

He quickly closed them.

A SWEEP THROUGH THE HOUSE CONFIRMED ZACH'S suspicions. The house's occupants had left in a hurry.

The coven had used the home as a dormitory and school house. Young witches had left open books in the ground-floor classroom. He'd remind himself later to feed the gerbil in the corner. The bedrooms, with bunks lining the walls, had clothes scattered across the floor.

As to whether they would return soon, he doubted it. Lark and her guardians were unknown quantities, and if the way those blood witches behaved around Lark was any indication, they *feared* her.

Or, at least, they feared what the serpent was capable of doing.

The events from the attack at the hideout yesterday flashed through his mind. He vividly recalled the horrific force that had smashed into his chest. The fallen hunters around him had nearly died.

What other powers did this serpent tattoo possess? He needed to learn sooner rather than later if he stood a chance of protecting Lark.

He returned to the kitchen to find Lark and Janet sitting on the barstools next to the rectangular, quartz-covered center island.

"You really need to get some sleep," Janet said. "You smell like you're about to pass out."

Lark slowly shook her head. "I know. I know. This whole situation is so overwhelming—the very thought of going to sleep jolts me awake."

Janet rolled her eyes. "You can't sleep because they put enough caffeine in their tea to keep a cow out to pasture for days." She stood and headed to the cabinets. Instead of rifling, she knew exactly where to go. "You don't hydrate properly, so we'll get some water in you while I hunt down a sleep aid."

"You don't have to do that." Lark smiled at Janet, then turned to see Zach staring at her. She licked her lips and drew her dark hair behind her ear. "I thought you'd left."

He strode into the kitchen. "I checked the house. It's clear."

An uncomfortable silence settled between them. Janet stood from her spot searching the lower cabinet. "I'm going to check the other rooms to see what I can find."

Lark gave her a don't-leave-me expression, but Janet missed it as she retreated.

"You just got here," Zach said. "Do you really trust them?"

"There's no safe place for me right now," Lark replied softly. "At least with these people, I have an idea where things stand. You and I don't have that kind of history."

He stiffened. "No, we don't have the best history."

The statement seemingly cast shadows on the well-lit room.

Zach continued. "I can't change what went down between us, but what I can do is show how much I care about you from this point forward." He didn't want to hear her rebuttal, so he walked out the door.

Might as well circle the house on guard duty and let the incoming freezing rain cool his heated blood.

Right outside the door, he heard her sniffle. The way she sucked in a breath before she cried. An all-too-familiar agony from their time in the hospital. The sounds shook him to the core.

Go in there. Fix this.

He took a step and stopped himself.

Through the window, he caught Janet's footsteps as she returned to the kitchen.

"Hey, you okay?" she asked.

"Oh yeah." Lark sniffed a couple of times. "I got my ass kicked at the diner and the parking garage. Now I'm a witch. It's all too much, to be honest."

He didn't move an inch. He should make things right between them, but if she didn't want him around, there was only so much he could do.

"Definitely," Janet replied. "Are you and Zach having problems? Seemed like you two needed some space."

"Don't worry about it."

"It's my job to worry." Janet sighed. "Do you still love him?"

Lark's annoyed groan punched his gut. "Our drama is that obvious, isn't it? I wish I still didn't care for him. Why does this love shit have to be so complicated?"

Relief filled him to hear she still cared about him, but he'd heard enough. Wasn't he supposed to be checking the perimeter?

A sweep over the back decks revealed a quiet glen. The frozen rain pelted the decks, the pitter-patter louder than he'd expected.

Lark's words followed him and pressed on the back of his neck while he focused on any movements in the woods. The nocturnal animals wouldn't emerge from their dens as the rain continued to nip at his skin.

Jamilah and Yolande continued their guard duty under an awning right outside the main house. Neither of their heads turned his way as he strolled past.

Either they didn't fear him, or they'd dealt with werewolves before. Hadn't Yolande called them *animals*?

His dad had often said similar words. Growing up, Zach would nod and often chime in with agreement. Now that he lived in a wolf's skin, the degradation didn't bounce off him as well. Hell, coming to terms with his sister's illness and accepting help from an alpha had given him a fresh perspective.

Zach rounded a corner to return to the front of the house. Brian stood in the middle of the path with a stiff back and hands clenched at his sides.

Here we go.

This wouldn't be the first or last time anyone stepped up to Zach, but this was the first time a wolf had done so.

Instead of weaving around Brian, he walked right up to him. Waited. Might as well let the guardian have his say.

Whether Zach would agree with his opinion was another matter.

Brian blinked as the frozen rain hit his face. His thick wool coat was already soaked through. His dark eyes briefly met Zach's—and interestingly enough, Brian's eyes trained on the house then refocused on Zach.

So it's like that between us, huh?

"I've only known Lark for a short time, but it's pretty clear you two used to be together, right?"

Zach didn't answer. Why bother? Brian knew what was up.

And it was also none of his damn business.

"This place feels like it's in the middle of nowhere," Brian said conversationally. "We're far enough from the Red hunters to stay under the radar. And holy shit. Did you see the way those witches brought us here?"

Zach shrugged.

Brian continued. "These are some serious fighters. I'm curious to see how they handle themselves."

Brian waited for a comment, but Zach said nothing.

Lark's guardian nodded casually. "Lark should be safe here for the time being—"

"If you've got a point to make," Zach interjected, "you should make it."

Brian rubbed the water off his face. "Lark doesn't need you anymore. She's got me and Janet. I believe the blood witches will protect her too. And one of them is her aunt. She'd be a lot happier if you left." He let his voice trail off, as if he'd made a solid argument.

Zach took another step forward, forcing Brian to retreat.

"You don't know me or my background, yet you're making a lot of assumptions." Zach put up one finger. "One, you're too trusting. Those witches just called us animals, and they're withholding critical information. If you were truly protecting her, like I want to do, you'd want help. Two, you don't have a lick of combat or ops training. Since you're a werewolf, you have two potential adversaries: hunters and the witches. You're not prepared for either of them."

Brian retreated a bit, then a hint of menace touched his features. "What if she asks you to leave? Would you go then?"

Zach held in a sigh. Had Brian heard him?

"I'll respect her wishes and keep my distance, but I refuse to leave her vulnerable until she's ready to take care of herself—and right now, you're not prepared. I could teach you, if you'd like?"

The tension in Brian's shoulders eased, but defiance still lined his frown.

"I'd rather see your back as you left," he said stiffly.

With a tilt of his chin, Zach gestured south. "Do you and I need to settle this matter in the woods?"

A hint of wolf flashed in Brian's dark eyes, but his hunger to dominate Zach fought with common sense.

With a swallowed curse, Brian withdrew to the trees. But he disappeared after Zach peered at him.

Zach could practically imagine Kaden's amused snort. The Windham alpha wouldn't have tolerated that type of behavior from a rogue, but Zach didn't have his brother-in-law's powerful presence.

Yet.

Zach returned to the back porch and waited in the growing shadows. While the wolf quieted under his skin, he considered his circumstances. Why hadn't he asked Kaden more questions? Observing werewolves' behavior was one thing, but living the life was another matter.

His racing heart steadied, but the wolf within him circled again and again. Restless. Hungry to fight for the territory that should be his.

Night fell and the frozen rain continued to fall. The ever-present sound of frogs and bleating crickets should've added a layer of serenity, but Zach remained vigilant.

Long ago, Jamilah and Yolande had ended their guard duty, and another set of witches had replaced them.

These houses still left him uneasy. A peculiar hum settled into his bones and rattled his sharpened senses. Every time he tried to peer out to the sea, the dark purple water wavered with an unnatural shimmer.

"It's the defensive measures that you don't see coming that are the most dangerous," his dad always said.

Until he fought on an even playing field with the witches, Zach would observe and learn.

The faint yawn of a window opening above his head caught his attention. Lark's scent floated down to him, drawing him from his sentry spot toward the porch's support column.

Her words echoed through his head.

I wish this love shit wasn't so complicated.

Ditto.

He loved her. That was certain, but he'd hurt her too. He wanted to pull her into his arms to show her he had no doubts. That he wouldn't make the same mistake he'd made before.

She closed the window, but her presence remained. Instead of heading to her window, he made his way to the back door, locking it behind him. The front door was still open, so he locked that too. He took the steps two at a time until he reached her closed door.

He was prepared to knock on her door and speak his piece.

He was prepared to apologize again and admit he should've kept in contact with her. If none of that worked, he'd consider what to do next.

But all that would have to wait.

Someone had snuck inside—without a sound—and had smeared a set of bloody words across her bedroom door: *Leave or soon this blood will be yours.*

[11]

The next morning didn't start well.

"So what you're saying is someone waltzed in here and did a paint-by-numbers job on my wall?" Lark placed her hands on her hips. Yolande's straight face annoyed her to high hell.

"We have protective wards around the house, but those wards were breached."

"Then who is still present on the grounds?" Zach asked from behind her.

Lark folded her arms and didn't turn around. So far this morning, she'd done well keeping space between them.

"I don't have the authority to reveal that information," Yolande said.

"Your coven members left this house in a hurry," Janet said. "Are any of them staying in the third house?"

"I don't have the authority to—" Yolande began.

"To reveal that information," Lark finished for her. "We got it. You're *not* going to help us."

"An investigation has already taken place, and when I

determine the culprit, we will handle the matter in-house," Yolande explained.

Lark approached Yolande. "I thought I would be safe here."

"You are relatively safe. But..." Yolande sighed. "But Folake is *impur*."

The serpent immediately translated the word: tainted. Impure. Unclean.

Yolande continued. "Many of us know firsthand what the snake is capable of doing. It's best you stay away from others until we determine how you plan to control it."

"Control it? Are you serious?" Lark asked.

Yolande's stony expression finally melted into a small smile. "If you haven't seen—or *heard*—its true intentions yet, you will soon enough." With that, the blood witch enforcer left the house.

Lark had heard the serpent's intention to harm others, but so far it had only protected her.

"What do we do now?" Janet asked as she washed the dishes from their breakfast.

"There's nothing we can do unless we find out who entered the house," Brian said. "If they've got security cameras, I doubt they'd let us see them."

"They know who did it," Zach said evenly.

Lark gave up trying to avoid him and faced him. He leaned against the island, arms crossed and expression broody. The hunter was present.

Zach continued. "All Yolande did was touch the blood, then she left. She didn't check for forced entry or question any of us."

Lark's guardians exchanged a worried glance.

"If I was in her position," Zach said, "I would confront the culprit and punish them, unless..."

"Unless what?" Janet asked.

"Unless she was the one who'd done it," he finished.

"I don't like any of this," Janet whispered.

"I don't either," Lark said, "but a couple more days won't hurt. I'm meeting my aunt at the main house to talk for a while. We should all be vigilant until I return."

"What time are you going?" Janet wiped off her hands on a dishtowel. "I'll go with you."

"I was told to come alone." Lark wanted to chuckle at Janet's pursed lips—her mother had done that when she was displeased. "Don't worry. I'll be careful. She is my aunt, after all."

LARK WALKED ALONE FROM THE LAKE HOUSE TO FIND her aunt waiting on the main house's back porch.

Iluminada still wore black attire, this time black trousers and a blouse, with a sweater over her shoulders.

"It's so cold out here," Lark said. "Why didn't you wait for me inside?"

Her aunt offered a bright smile, and delight filled Lark. "I couldn't wait. We've been apart for too long."

Iluminada wrapped her arms around Lark's shoulders and hugged her. The gesture caught Lark off guard, but no one had hugged her like that in a while.

"I can see Lupita in you," her aunt murmured. "I miss her so much."

Abruptly, she released Lark. "Sorry about that. Let me get you inside." She slipped her arm around Lark's and drew her indoors. A tingle danced along her spine, and she turned around to see Zach watching them from the Lake House. She pushed thoughts of him away and followed her aunt into the house.

Iluminada offered to take her coat in the mudroom, but

Lark found the house to be too chilly. "I'll wear it until I warm up."

"Of course." Iluminada leaned toward Lark with a mischievous smile. "Zenobia has one foot in the grave. During the wintertime, this place feels like a tomb. C'mon."

She beckoned Lark through a hallway to the stairwell. At the top of the stairs, they walked past several sets of closed doors. None of them were marked.

"How many people live here?" Lark asked.

"A few."

At the end of the hall, right next to an alcove with a window, was an end table and a few potted plants. Two rubber plants took up most the table, while a defiant orchid gave a splash of purple, white, and yellow. Lovely. Compared to the lack of greenery throughout the house, this tiny space felt like back home with her parents. Lark's mom had loved plants.

Had Iluminada placed these here?

She led Lark into a cozy bedroom with tall rafter ceilings, a seating area with cloth-covered couches, and a queen-sized bed in another corner. Two windows next to the seating area didn't provide much light due to the gloomy conditions outside, but lamps—with a plant beside each one—lit the room here and there.

Lark walked in, marveling at the mustard-yellow walls and hand-woven rugs on the hardwood floors. Watercolor paintings of the sea and forest adorned the walls. Yep, Iluminada had to be the feisty gardener in the house.

Just like Mom.

Speaking of her mother, Lark noticed a sepia-toned photo in a weathered frame. Three dark-haired girls sat next to each other on a porch swing. Their dresses whispered of another decade, but their smiles were timeless. Mama's mischievous grin shone from the girl in the middle, while

Iluminada was the lanky girl to the left. Who sat to their right? That particular girl, with a pointed chin and harsh smile, hadn't wanted her picture taken.

"Who are they?"

"Come over here. That's the troublesome trio. Me, your mama, and Justine."

That made Lark pause. "You grew up with Justine?"

She nodded. "No matter how hard Lupita and I tried to include Jussie in friendship, she always had a darkness about her. Through her studies of blood witch history she came to believe many fallacies." She sighed. "Let's not talk about Jussie." Iluminada urged Lark to sit on the chair next to the couch. "There's something very special I wanted to share with you."

"What is it?" Lark joined her aunt, who presented a tiny gold-plated box.

"This was your mother's," Iluminada explained. "Now it belongs to you."

Lark's brow furrowed as she took in the rectangular box. Instead of words across the surface, she spied ornate swirls and indentations. She brushed her fingers across the top. No, the indentations weren't random. They rose and fell in a pattern. Like waves.

Iluminada placed the box on her lap then slid off the top, revealing a set of five needles nestled into slots. "This is a witch's bloodletting box."

Lark forced herself not to cringe. When she'd first heard the name "blood witches," she hadn't connected bloodletting with them. Yet this all had to be true. Phoebe's attack yesterday hadn't been an illusion.

They really did cut themselves to release their power.

Lark peered at the needles again. The scent of nutmeg wafted from inside. Shouldn't it smell antiseptic?

Iluminada presented her hands, palms up. "The serpent

demon is inked under your skin, but you're still a witch, Lark. So you must know our ways and understand them." Her face went from warm to serious. "Everything begins with blood. Your life. My life. And sometimes death. The greatest gift one witch can give another is to keep our blood clean." She used a fingertip to tilt up Lark's chin. "You will never see a human man out in the open here."

"Why?"

"Men pollute a blood witch's magic over time. Therefore, we keep our distance unless"—Iluminada quirked a grin —"we want a little bit of company."

That made Lark chuckle. Briefly, she pondered how were-wolves fit into this equation.

"Women like me can perform blood magic, but once you have the tattoo, you can't anymore. But the day may come where you'll be free. Maybe you'll find Folake and return her little gift."

The news rocketed through Lark. "You mean I can *force* her to take it back?"

"Shh. Not so loud. I shouldn't have told you that, but yes, *kindred spirits* are witches that share similar blood. They can pass the demon from one to the other. It's very, very rare for us to find a kindred blood witch."

"But if you're my aunt, why didn't she give it to you…"

"I might be your kin, but that doesn't mean I am her match. Unfortunately, she is yours."

Now that she knew the truth, the urge to go out and confront that horrible woman made Lark stand, but her aunt caught her arm.

"If you're doing what I think you're doing," Iluminada said gently, "you're not ready to face her. Or Justine."

"She left me with this thing," Lark said.

"Folake never wanted to be found all these years, and I doubt you'll find her now. Before she received the tattoo from another witch, she was well trained in the craft. Do you believe you're ready to face her?"

Lark swallowed deeply. She was in no condition to face anyone. She still hadn't recovered from her concussion.

Iluminada patted the box. "Master the blood craft. Be prepared."

Lark surrendered. For now. "What do I have to do?"

Iluminada grasped her right hand. "You should meet and accept pain. A blood witch's welcome companion. First, the index finger." She held tight to Lark's digit, which she pricked, and Lark held still. A droplet of blood quickly formed.

The tattoo shifted on her back.

"This is raw power," her aunt intoned. "But you need more than this tiny drop to destroy entire armies. With the right glyph, a witch shedding enough blood can kill you where you stand. Anticipate their actions. You may have to use the serpent to save your life."

$$[\ 12\ ]$$

After Lark was safely inside the house, Zach waited for her to emerge. Yolande approached him.

"I need your assistance," she said.

"How?" And why should he offer it?

"This morning, Jamilah reported that the Red hunting clan has gotten too close to our property."

Zach nodded. "They have training grounds on the island."

"I know, but they've never gotten close to the wards before…or left their own cameras nearby."

Now that got his attention. "When do you want to leave?" he asked.

"How about now?" Brian waltzed out the back door of the house and joined them.

"Lark is still inside," Zach said. "Are you sure you want to leave?"

Brian crossed his arms. His short, curly black hair was still wet from a shower. "The blood witches will protect her, and we won't be gone long, right?" he asked Yolande.

"Of course," she replied. "There are wards everywhere."

Which were not so helpful last night, he thought.

After Zach made sure he had everything for a reconnaissance mission, he relayed their task to Janet.

"I'll wait for Lark and text you when she returns," Janet reassured him.

The trio set out southward on foot. Brian tried to keep a brisk pace, but Zach slowed down for the witch to keep up. Moving too quickly through territory with trained trackers wouldn't be too wise either.

"How far do we need to go?" Brian asked. "It looks like no one has been through here in ages."

Zach frowned and pointed to broken brush a few yards from them. "Hikers walked through here at least a couple days ago."

At Brian's confused expression, Zach pointed out the smudged footprints.

"They went off-trail and headed west back to the coastline," he explained.

"How do you know those weren't hunters?" Brian asked.

"One set was made from sneakers and another one from hiking boots," Zach explained. "Hunters from a clan are issued military-grade gear from a trusted manufacturer."

Brian nodded.

"If I see a hunter's footprint," he said. "I'll let you know so you can remember it."

"Thanks." Brian didn't sound thankful, though.

So far, the tension between them was manageable. Zach could be a dick about Brian's power play, but Zach's situation had changed. Saving Cyn had changed him. *Adapt or suffer the consequences,* he'd learned. He was one of them now, and if he wanted to survive, that meant working with werewolves to keep them alive too.

They continued southward until Zach noticed a road through the trees.

Yolande turned to them then glanced around.

"Do you need help finding something?" Zach asked her.

The blood witch edged closer to them. "I had to make sure I was safely outside of the coven's wards to speak to you."

He'd been right to be suspicious about the coven's secrets.

"You're all in danger if you stay. If I were you, I'd leave as soon as possible," she whispered.

"Are you the one who left the blood on her wall?" Brian asked.

"No, it wasn't me," she said, "but I agree with the message."

Brian snorted.

"Why is Lark in danger?" Zach asked.

"If Justine can't make her underlings bring Lark to her, she'll come herself." Yolande's heart rate shot up like a frightened rabbit and her steady demeanor vanished. "One powerful blood witch after another will attack us."

Zach surveyed the sky through the trees while he absorbed the weight of her words. "If we leave tonight, will Justine still chase after us?"

She nodded.

He carefully considered his next question. "Do we stand a better chance if we stay here?"

Yolande grimaced, then reluctantly nodded. "You *still* shouldn't stay here."

"Why?" Zach asked. "If you witches have all these powers, you'll also have a better chance at winning."

She glanced away then refocused on them. "My daughter was one of the witchlings that had to escape yesterday."

Brian's eyebrows rose as he caught the gist of what she meant.

"I can't protect her home," Yolande said, "or give her a place to return to if Justine destroys it."

"She's that powerful?" Brian asked. "Even with your defenses? You guys can do *magic*!"

She sighed. "Justine's offensive strength is unimaginable. She knows many deadly, rare spells. We're talking catastrophic destruction."

Brian tried to speak again, but Zach shot his hand out to silence him.

"We're not asking the *right* questions," Zach said slowly. "If what you're saying is true, and Lark is a threat to all of us, why does Justine want to kill her? If we knew why, maybe we could convince her to end all of this."

Yolande slowly shook her head. "Never negotiate with a religious zealot, Wolf. Justine has come to believe she can save the sisterhood." Her frown deepened. "She believes all the demons will vanish from this plane of existence if she *kills* the most powerful one of them all: the serpent demon."

[13]

After leaving her aunt's private quarters with a spell book and the bloodletting kit in hand, Lark explored the rest of the house. Now that the blood enforcers no longer followed her every footstep, she was free to see what other secrets the blood witches kept.

After getting pushed into the deep side of an abyss that seemingly never ended, she was still in shock.

Magic exists. I have powers.

She clutched the glyph book tighter. Even if she couldn't cast the spells in the book, she wanted to understand what the witches were capable of.

As she walked down the hallway to the stairwell, she flicked through the pages. None of them made sense…yet.

Someday, she'd find Folake. And that bitch would put up a fight using magic to prevent Lark from giving it back.

She had to be ready.

At the bottom of the steps, she walked into the great room to find it empty. Shouldn't she have expected that after everyone had fled? She strolled deeper into the room and headed to the wall of bookcases at the other end.

Delight tickled her spine as she read the titles she couldn't see before. Text in Latin wavered and flashed to become English: *Diseases of the Blood*; *Transfusion Techniques and Approaches*. Another row had medical books in French, while another had chemistry textbooks in Russian. Why bother with Google when she had everything she needed here?

So much knowledge sat on these shelves. Any of these could be the stepping stones to help her in the future.

If only she had more time in the world.

She leaned down to check out the bottom row. A brand-new leather-bound book stood out from the other worn ones. The title caught her eye: *Wound Care Best Practices*.

She'd seen this book before back home—but that one had a ragged spine and pages with creases from someone marking their reading spot. Had Mama taken one of the books from here when she'd left?

Halfway across the room, a faint breeze tickled the side of her face. Now where did that come from? She leaned to the right and left until she could detect the source. The air came from a thin seam from between the bookcases. She had to strain to see it, but once she put her hand up to the division between the bookcases, the snake across her back came to life.

Yes, something was there, but did she truly want to find out what other secrets the witches kept?

Before Lark had left the main house, Iluminada had invited her to return for dinner.

"You should break bread with us," she'd said.

After the invitation, Lark had returned to the Lake House feeling elated, so why did doubt press on her temples as she stood outside of the main house's dining room?

Was she dressed appropriately? She'd removed her bandage, washed her hair, and worn one of the sweater dresses she'd found in the bedroom she slept in last night. The garment was a few sizes too big, but she'd rather swim in a dress than wear a tight one. Most clothes she found swallowed her small chest.

She stepped into the formal dining room to find a table with twelve seats, but only six place settings had been prepared.

Zenobia held court at the head of the table, while Iluminada waved at Lark from her left.

"I was afraid you wouldn't come." Iluminada beckoned her again.

To Zenobia's right, a witch Lark hadn't met before peered at her. The dark-skinned woman had sharp, light brown eyes, but the soft smile she offered was welcoming. She wore similar black clothing as the others, but it was less formfitting and loose-flowing for her larger bosom. The light from the candles on the table reflected off the jewelry she wore. Pearl earrings adorned her earlobes, while gold rings sparkled from her nose and lip.

She was regal without words.

To the Black woman's right, Yolande greeted Lark.

"Good evening," she said. Her straight strawberry-blonde hair was pinned in a severe bun. A pearl barrette softened her harsh expression.

Lark took the chair next to her aunt. Once she was settled into her seat with her napkin in her lap, just like Aunt Iluminada, Jamilah emerged from the kitchen with plates of food.

Jamilah gently set a bowl of lobster bisque in front of Zenobia, but her cohort Yolande got the cold treatment.

When Jamilah got to the other side of the table, Lark sighed. As much as she wanted to spend time with her aunt, she missed the laughter and lighter conversation with Zach, Janet and Brian. As she'd left the Lake House, Zach had finished cooking fish tacos.

Not that she didn't love lobster—especially fresh seafood —but who didn't enjoy homemade tacos? Her mouth had watered watching Janet prepare fresh guacamole.

"Are you alright?" Iluminada asked her.

Lark smiled. "I'd hoped our dinner would be less formal," she whispered.

Her aunt chuckled and leaned toward her. "Zenobia is stuck in her ways and not everyone appreciates her traditions, but she has touched each of us. She'll grow on you too."

She nodded. Each witch regarded the elder witch with respect. As much as she missed the comradery with her friends, she had an opportunity to explore her mother's life. The sooner she understood the witches' way of life, the more comfortable she'd become.

SLEET AND THICK CLOUDS PARTIALLY OBSCURED THE moon, but the view from the loft in the Lake House to the sea was still breathtaking.

Lark had turned off all the lights and let the shadows take over the space.

Beyond the double window, the ocean swayed and undulated. Growing up in Vancouver, Lark had seen such a sight many times. Both in the light and the dark—but this time, with the serpent gliding along her skin in a lazy crawl from the base of her spine up to her neck, the view materialized in a fashion she hadn't witnessed before. With each inch the tat crawled, the peculiar waves revealed their secrets. She released the latch on the window and slid the pane upward.

Gusts of wind, along with the soothing sounds of crashing waves against the small pier in front of the house, filled the loft.

She stared into the darkness, hoping to confirm her suspicions. Then it appeared. A line of demarcation, shimmering and strange, flashed before her eyes.

What was she seeing? More magic?

"It's beautiful, isn't it?" said a deep voice behind her.

She didn't glance over her shoulder as Zach joined her on the bay window seat and leaned against the wall.

"On any other day, I'd call it familiar, but tonight I feel like my eyes are playing tricks on me."

He scooted closer to her to look out the window, and his presence caught her off guard. With him sitting right next to her, she couldn't help but steal a glance at him.

If he was still wounded, he didn't show it. He no longer leaned to the right to protect his side. Had he recovered fully?

She followed the line of his jaw. A shadow had formed on his chin. For a man who always shaved, seeing Zach McGinnis rough around the edges made him darker. More appealing.

"I was out on patrol with Yolande today, and she told me they have protective wards that extend out to the ocean," he replied. "Maybe you're seeing those."

Jealousy ate at her. "What were you doing out on patrol with her?"

"There was *something* she wanted Brian and me to see along the border to the property. We need to be vigilant in the days to come, but I don't want you to worry about the problem yet."

She nodded, but curiosity remained. What was that *something* Yolande wanted them to see?

He folded his arms behind his head. He was close enough for her to see the steady rise and fall of his wide chest. How she wished she could rest her head there. Listen to his heartbeat to lull her to sleep.

"What's on your mind?" he asked. "You're tense."

She swallowed past the lump in her throat. "You remember when we used to sit at that diner next to the hospital? The one with the awful coffee, but the best full breakfast?"

"Yeah."

"Right now, I feel like I'm still sitting there. Waiting for the tsunami to hit, but unsure how high the waves will be."

"We came here for answers, and we have some."

"We do, but…I can't help but feel like the worst is waiting out there. Like back at the diner." She snorted. "Now that I think about it, all we did was wait there for shitty news. Disappointing CAT scans. Heartbreaking blood results. It was like there was a dark cloud hovering over that place."

"It wasn't all bad news," he said softly as he leaned toward her and touched the side of her face. She soaked in the warmth. "And you got to rest. Real rest. You fell asleep every time you ate that big-ass breakfast."

That made her release a full-bellied laugh. Good God, he remembered. She hadn't believed him when he'd told her she crashed hard after she ate. Until he snapped the infamous pic.

"My mouth was *wide* open." She sighed.

After seeing herself fast asleep in the picture, she'd threatened bodily harm if he didn't delete it, but that only goaded him further.

"You're about to go viral, baby," he'd said. *"I'm holding this as blackmail to show our grandkids."*

They'd had good times.

"I thought it was cute." Zach rested his hand against her leg, only to release it when she glanced at him.

"Sorry." He paused. "No, I'm not sorry I did that."

"I liked it," she admitted. "It felt nice. I've been alone too often. Even when Aunt Gretchen tried to make me spend the holidays with them I didn't."

"Why didn't you?"

"'Cause I was *tired* all the time. It was easier to work and earn money so I could reopen The Hunting Grounds than… to live."

"Oh, Lark." He edged closer until they sat side by side. His rising heat bathed her. Like a cat, she wanted to stretch out over him. Lose herself in it. "You were supposed to stay in Vancouver and live on. What happened to grad school?"

Too many things happened over that year: her dad's passing, Zach leaving, and the Azzurro Clan collapsing without her dad's guidance.

She bit her lower lip hard. "I quit. It was for the best."

"Best for who?"

"I don't know, to be honest." She expected him to push harder—Dad had stressed he'd wanted her to be able to support herself with a comfortable job. Even if she did love working with him at the pub.

The evening stretched out, and the shadows grew hazy as sleep pressed on her. Her head drooped to the left, before settling on a comfortable pillow to her right. This particular pillow steadily rose and fell like the waves outside, lulling her to the rest she needed.

[14]

Lark woke up after the best sleep ever. Just about as good as post-sex sleep.

Maybe.

Now, the fact that she slumbered next to Zach was another matter.

Her head no longer ached. The bruises along her back and arms didn't bother her anymore. Her left arm was draped over his chest, while the rest of her was curled up on his lap. There was something tranquil about the thrum of his slowly beating heart under her arm. The way his chin rested against the top of her head and his arms wrapped around her, offering security.

Was he still sleeping?

His hardening erection under her butt told her otherwise.

She rolled her eyes and shifted, but he didn't let her go.

"I might be a werewolf now," he murmured, "but I'm still a man."

She caught the smile in his words, even without seeing his face.

She tried not to wiggle against his hard length, but the

yearning to have him touch her deepened until her thighs clenched and her breath quickened.

He nuzzled the top of her head, and goodness help her— he tilted his hips upward. "You smell so damn good right now."

Why did he have to say that? She clutched his shoulders and forced herself to stand. As much as she wanted—needed —to bottle this feeling and carry it with her for the rest of the day, she also needed time to sort out her feelings.

Being with him, wanting him, all of those things felt right. Just like they used to.

She took a step back and faked a smile. She'd worry about werewolves and death another day.

"You probably need to go to the bathroom," she said.

"I'll be fine. You needed the rest."

"C'mon, Z. You still drink enough water for twenty people."

He rolled his eyes and quickly stood. "Yeah, I do gotta go."

The morning passed, but the stillness and quiet among the houses disappeared as children and women arrived from the woods. Lark peered out the window as they ambled up to the house.

Why hadn't they arrived by car?

"Who are they?" Janet whispered from behind her. Even Brian wanted to check them out over Janet's shoulder.

Unable to resist seeing them face to face, Lark headed out the back door to the courtyard. Janet and Brian trailed after.

The sea of adult and youthful faces represented every color, shape, and size, and the kids ranged from toddlers to teenagers. All their faces showed doubt and fear. Only a few had backpacks—hadn't they left in a hurry before she'd arrived?

Witchlings, she recalled one of the elders saying. All of

them were learning the things her mother hadn't lived to show her.

"It's her!" one of the older witchlings cried.

A few kids scrambled back, but the adults reassured them as Lark made her way to them with her hands up.

"It's okay," Lark said softly. "I won't hurt you."

"Sylvia!" Yolande called from the main house porch. She got down on one knee, and a red-haired girl rushed to her.

"Mama!" She jumped into Yolande's arms.

"I got you."

Lark turned back to the children. Six women tried to usher them toward the third house, while Fredda, the regal woman Lark met at dinner yesterday, strode up to her.

"We'd hoped you'd stay in the house," she said with a wistful expression.

"I know." Lark pointed back to the Lake House. "Why aren't they going back to their home? I can switch with them."

The Black woman grinned. "That's kind of you and all, but there's a reason you're in the witchling dormitory."

"But all their classroom and belongings are in here."

Fredda gestured for Lark to follow her back to the Lake House. Once she reached one of the light blue walls, she patted the surface. "There are special spells on the Lake House to track the occupants."

Lark snorted. "That way you'll know if I become a problem."

"You got it." Fredda walked into the Lake House, and Lark followed. Her guardians remained on the porch.

Fredda checked the fridge and then ran her finger along the counter. "You keep a clean house. Good. I didn't want the witchlings' caregivers to come in here and see you threw a party or two." She gave Lark a wink.

Lark hid a smile. "It's not hard. I know how to take care of myself."

"I see." Fredda shed her coat and placed it over one of the chairs.

Lark glanced through the window to see the elders leaving the Mountain Haven House to where the witchlings went.

"Are you here to ensure I behave while the kids get settled in?"

"More or less." Fredda shrugged, then gave Lark a long look she couldn't read. "To be honest, I might not be able to hold you here even if I wanted to."

"The serpent…" Lark let the words trail off.

Fredda nodded. "When you arrived, I was surprised to see you still had guardians—much less werewolves. I haven't had a guardian in a long time."

Lark took a seat on one of the island chairs. "You have a tattoo also?"

"Yes, I got mine when I turned seventeen during World War II." At Lark's confused expression, she added, "The demons prolong our lives. I was born in the 1920s."

Lark's stomach plummeted to her feet. Damn, if she survived, she'd have elongated life with this thing? She was glad she'd decided to sit down.

That poor woman must've lost her guardians to one of the many horrible events in the past. "I'm so sorry. They didn't die of old age, did they? I'm assuming they were humans."

Fredda glanced away as she considered what to say. Lark had never liked when her dad hid his feelings from her.

"They were humans." Fredda paused. "Fragile and delicate. They always are until you don't need them anymore."

Lark's brow knitted. "What do you mean?"

Fredda took a deep breath. "I didn't want to be the one

to tell you this, but every demon summons guardians to protect them from the mortal world, yet the demons are corrupt. Never forget that. They'd bite off their own leg to feed their desire for suffering."

The way Lark had attacked those men came to mind. "I have an idea what you mean."

"The serpent has spoken to you."

"Yes, and the message wasn't pretty."

Fredda's expression grew wistful as she approached Lark. "The messages will grow uglier and uglier. They only want you to see the darkness, even when you're searching for the light." Fredda grasped her hand, and Lark found her skin smooth and warm.

"Don't be like me. Don't listen to it." Fredda's gaze flicked to the window and the guardians sitting on the stairs. "Don't kill them like I did mine."

Lark froze, her heart caught in her throat. Then she turned to Janet and Brian, hoping they hadn't heard. The pair hadn't moved and still kept watch.

"I'm stronger than I look," Lark said firmly to Fredda. Maybe she'd wanted to hear herself say it out loud. "And I'm not alone. Zach would never let me become like that either."

Fredda gave her a knowing grin. "You must mean the handsome wolf you arrived with? The elders find him fascinating. He isn't like werewolves I've met over the years, like your guardians."

"I doubt he would be. He's a werewolf that used to be a werewolf hunter."

Fredda laughed. "That explains everything. Not to say all werewolves are like your guardians, but the few I've encountered aren't as refined, yet sharp around the edges, as your *friend*."

Lark rolled her eyes. "It's not like that between us—well, it used to be."

Fredda put her hands on her hips. "But not anymore, you're saying?"

"I keep telling everyone we're 'complicated,' and even I'm tired of saying that."

"Complicated… The witchling caregivers spotted him guarding the houses. Avril said he reminded her of a lickable Jared Padalecki. I'm not familiar with the actor, but I guess Zach's fair game?"

Heat filled Lark's face. "Now, I didn't say all that."

"I'll be sure to broadcast to the whole coven that your hunter is available for any trysts."

"Fredda, you seem pretty cool, but…not so much now."

She missed having friends. It was hard to foster relationships when you worked the night and weekend shifts. Before she'd known Fredda's true age, Lark would've assumed the woman was no more than twenty-five.

"Other than your non-announcement, what are the plans for today?" Lark asked. "Do the caregivers need to fetch anything?"

"They probably will want to come in later, but don't worry about it." Fredda's calm expression hardened. "We all need to prepare ourselves for Justine and her people."

Lark nodded. "What should I do? Other than stay out of the way."

"Good question. I heard Iluminada taught you a thing or two about blood magic."

"Just the basics. She even gave me a book of blood glyphs, but none of them worked."

"The glyphs are good to know," Fredda explained, "but they are useless in our hands." "Our magic comes through the demon tattoos."

As if on cue, one of the caregivers approached the house. Lark's guardians spoke to the woman and then got of the way.

"Come find me later," Fredda whispered.

Fredda met the caregiver at the back door. Lark stood and smiled, expecting an introduction, but the dark-haired woman swept past her and hurried out of the kitchen. Fredda mouthed, "Sorry," to her.

Lark shook her head. It wasn't Fredda's fault they feared her. Lark had to be the one to set the record straight.

Somehow.

She didn't have long to sit with a cold cup of tea in the kitchen before Brian entered the house, with Janet behind him.

Lark smiled at them. Step one in doing the right thing would be to set her guardians free. If Justine was coming, they'd be in danger.

"Hey, you two," she said. "I'm glad you came inside. We need to talk."

The morose expressions on their faces made her smile die. Had something happened?

"Yes, we do," Brian said firmly. "Do you mind a short walk?"

"Only if you're feeling up to it," Janet added.

"I'm good." Lark was better than good. Zach had probably healed her while she'd slept in his arms. "Let's go and hurry back."

Lark donned her coat and headed out into the woods with them. She didn't see Zach anywhere, but she had a feeling he wasn't far away.

"What's on your mind?" she asked once they could no longer see the coven's houses.

"When were you going to tell us the truth?" Brian said bitterly.

"About what?" How much had they overheard?

"We heard you talking to the witch," Janet said with less fire than Brian.

"You mean about the guardians?" Lark sighed. "Look, I planned to—"

"No, we want to know why Zach didn't outright tell us he's a hunter." Brian stopped walking, and Lark was forced to move to not bump into him.

Lark folded her arms. Why hadn't Z told them? She had an idea. "He's not a hunter anymore. The minute he became a werewolf, that door closed for good."

"They may not want him back, but do you honestly believe years of loyalty to a clan vanishes overnight?" Brian asked.

"That's a good question," she admitted. "I don't know."

"He has been nothing but kind to us," Janet said as Brian shook his head in disgust. "But if he's put into a situation where he must choose between a hunter's life and a were-wolf's life, what would he do?"

The right thing, Lark immediately thought.

"Back when I knew him as a hunter," Lark said slowly, "he never made me believe he wasn't a man of character."

He'd still left her, but now that she knew what he'd done to save his sister's life, she had no doubt he'd sacrifice his own life to do what needed to be done.

She opened her mouth to tell them Zach's tale, but thought better of it. This wasn't her story to tell.

Instead she said, "Do you trust me?"

Janet and Brian glanced at each other.

"Of course we do," Brian said. "I have never felt like I belonged before. I went from one miserable job, one hiding spot to another, but now I have you and Janet."

Janet smiled at him. "You're not the pack's runt, you know."

"I quit my job at the firm last night," he admitted.

"You did?" A few days had passed. So much had

happened. Lark cursed. Why hadn't she thought about their personal lives?

"This is my home now," he said.

She glanced at Janet. Maybe Lark could spare Janet from abandoning her life in Vancouver. "Did you quit too?"

"I made the call two days ago." She gave Lark a half-smile. "You didn't make this choice. We did. We want to be here."

"But what about your *life*? Don't you have anyone who will worry about you?"

The pair exchanged a pained look.

"I had a couple of friends," Janet said, "but without a pack, I wasn't close to any of them."

"My girlfriend dumped me a month ago," Brian whispered. "If Claire were still around, I'd think differently."

That made Lark cringe. "Sorry."

Brian gave her a brave face. "That's in the past. We're all together now, and I wouldn't be doing my job unless I protected you from him. You might trust him, but it's my job to anticipate problems—"

"She likes him, you idiot," Janet said. "It's not that simple."

Brian sighed. "Doesn't matter. He's a risk. And if she doesn't have the heart to get rid of him, then I can do it."

"Don't do it." What a day to be dealing with these kinds of problems. "As much as I appreciate you both, I don't want you to get hurt. This is serious. You might *die*."

Brian snorted. "Trying to get rid of us won't make the problem go away."

Lark gave them a dark look. "No and Justine will still come for me, but I can't in good conscious let you two throw your lives away for me. The stakes are too high."

Janet and Brian glanced at each other. Their determined

expressions practically screamed she couldn't change their minds no matter how hard she tried.

"How about this?" Lark sighed. "Think about it for a couple of days. If you have a change of heart, I'll help you return to the mainland."

She waited for one of them to give in, but Janet took Lark's hand. "I can't believe you came outside without gloves again. Let's return to the house before you catch a cold."

Lark held back a laugh. "I haven't caught a cold since I was twelve."

"Good for you, then." Janet tugged her hard. "We'll cut off the frostbitten parts with scissors."

Lark still wanted them to leave. If one of them died, their death would be on her hands—and yet she couldn't deny they made her feel safe like her parents did back when she was a kid.

As they approached the house, Brian slowed down as if he was looking for someone. Probably Zach. Damn, not only did Lark have Justine to contend with, but she had a looming mutiny on her hands, too.

AFTER A LONG NIGHT HOLDING LARK, ZACH COULDN'T shake the restless feeling in his gut. They'd parted on good terms, but he couldn't wait to see her again. He could still feel her weight pressed against him as he ran through the forest. Could smell the sweet scent off the top of her head. Even chasing after winter cottontails or searching for any signs of the Red hunting clan did nothing to ease his longing.

If she had let him, he would've held her for far longer. Hell, he would've gladly waited until the sun set again to see her sleep soundly.

What has she done to me? he thought.

With nothing else left to do, he returned to the house to find Janet and Brian cooking lunch. The delicious smell of ham and bean soup filled the kitchen. His stomach growled in response. He hadn't eaten that in a long time.

Janet used a wooden spoon to stir the food in the pot while Brian prepared a salad. Neither of them glanced his way or acknowledged his presence.

"Any problems in the house while I was gone?" he asked as he took off his gloves and hat.

It took a full thirty seconds before Janet answered, "No."

Brian's back was turned to him, while Janet's profile revealed little, but signs that something was up lay in other signals. Janet's heartbeat picked up. Not in excitement, but fear. Under the delicious aroma of the soup, a new scent of sour sweat from Brian slithered through the room.

More apprehension.

Brian clutched the tongs hard enough to bend the metal. Zach sighed and took a spot at the kitchen dinette in the far corner of the room. It was the best vantage point to see every exit.

Ten minutes later, Janet gathered bowls, only two of them—then grabbed a third one. She arranged the soup bowls in front of the counter stools, along with spoons and napkins.

Brian fetched smaller bowls and dished out salad into each. Neither of them said a word as they sat down next to each other.

The third bowl was on the other side of the long rectangular island opposite them.

Interesting.

Zach got up. Instead of walking directly to the third place setting, he took the long way around the island and passed behind them.

If someone wanted to attack him, he'd rather they do it to his face versus his back.

But no one made such a move.

Good, he was hungry.

He took a seat, even arranging the napkin in his lap and taking a long drink from the glass of water in front of the soup bowl.

Janet and Brian had yet to touch their food.

Zach had experienced situations far tenser than this one so he eased back against the stool's back. "This is not the time for dissension," he said quietly. "Trouble is coming unlike any of us has seen before. If there's a problem, you need to say it."

Janet stared at the steam rising from her bowl while Brian struggled to keep himself in check. Finally, he turned to Zach with a glare dark enough to singe the skin on his back.

The thuds of someone bounding up the back porch steps made everyone focus on the door.

Yolande came inside. "We got a problem. Where's Lark?" The blood enforcer left the kitchen yelling Lark's name.

"Justine's here already?" Zach stood as Yolande returned.

"Yes, they're close by, but our other problem is just as bad." The enforcer's calm demeanor had fractured a little. "If we don't take the proper precautions, it could be worse."

Lark hurried into the room, her hair messy, as if she'd taken a nap. "What's going on?"

"We got major problems," Yolande said. "Justine's people have breached the wards to the south."

"They're here," Lark said as her face grew pale.

"The wolves will investigate the breach," Zach said. "How far?"

"About half a mile south." Yolande turned to Lark. "We need you at the main house. A box with demons trapped inside has arrived."

[15]

With only the tales she'd heard from Iluminada and Zenobia to warn her, Lark had no idea what she'd face.

And why did they need her?

She was a blood witch, but she didn't know any of the necessary ceremonies or rituals.

What she did appreciate was having Zach by her side as they walked up to the main house. He was ready to go to the breach point but insisted on escorting her. Brian and Janet waited in the woods.

Lark shook her hands to shake out the nerves. Beside her, Zach was steady as usual in his body armor.

Right outside the back door, Zach paused.

"Do you feel that?" he whispered. He clutched her arm. "Maybe you shouldn't go in there."

"What are you feeling?" She didn't feel strange at all. Matter of fact, her tattoo lay still for once.

Yolande turned to Lark. "From now on, the animals should keep their distance. The box has an effect on some of them."

There was that *animal* word again.

"Be careful out there." Lark pushed him back down the steps to make her point. "Don't do anything stupid."

That got a devilish grin out of him.

She turned to go inside but glanced over her shoulder. He'd slipped away into the night already.

Once in the great room, Lark found Zenobia and Fredda standing outside an open door—in the place where one of the bookcase panels should have stood.

A secret door, she mused.

"Lark, come join us, my dear," Zenobia said.

As quickly as Yolande fetched her, the enforcer backed away and escaped down the hallway.

"Yolande said a demon box had arrived," Lark said.

"Yes, and we must secure it before problems arise." The calm expression on Zenobia's face made Lark's stomach churn with discomfort.

Fredda beckoned her through the doorway into a small room with nothing more than a ladder leading down. A simple wooden box, about half a foot by half a foot, sat in the corner. The strange symbols on the sides had been etched by hand. She blinked, and the box's surface *changed*. What she'd believed were unfamiliar symbols transformed before her eyes to become English words.

She was seeing through the snake's eyes again: *We bind you in light. We bind you in blood. Return to the dark. Return to the gloom forevermore.*

After reading the symbols, Lark forced herself to breathe. How could such a simple thing be so deadly?

Zenobia stooped before the box and then wrapped it up using a red silk scarf with more symbols sewn into the fabric. On the side of her neck, a tentacle undulated upward to brush against her cheek before it crept back down.

Lark's once-still tattoo shifted until it sat on her chest. Its weight shouldn't have bothered her—so why did it become difficult for her to breathe?

"Let's go," Fredda whispered.

They descended the ladder into another room, far colder, with stone walls and pedestals holding candles. Fredda hurried to light them.

Lark shivered from the cold and waited near the ladder while Zenobia placed the box on a wooden pedestal in the center of the room. "We should begin the binding ceremony as soon as possible. Tonight, if we can."

Fredda nodded. "And security?"

Zenobia smiled at Lark. "We've got that covered thanks to our new sister."

Did she really expect Lark to stand guard down here in the dark and cold? Lark placed one hand on a rung, but Zenobia was on her in an instant.

"Are you crazy? I'm not staying here!" Lark said.

Fredda chuckled. "You thought we meant you? Don't worry. We have other options."

"And what do those options have to do with me?" She might as well get to the point.

"We are a shunned coven," Zenobia said. "The Owl Coven would rather leave their broken trash here for us to deal with it. So deal with it we must." She circled Lark, then drew her arm around Lark's shoulders. "The sisterhood draws power from working together, and now you must help us."

Dread soured Lark's stomach and the serpent on her skin slid down her belly in response. "How?"

"We are able to resist the blood demons in this box because we have demon tattooes," Zenobia said. "You could say we are no longer *open for business*—but the other blood witches nearby are vulnerable to their call. To keep everyone safe, we employ werewolves to handle the box."

The implications threatened to steal her breath. "So they don't hear its call?"

"Oh, they can hear it." When Lark tried to retreat, Zenobia's grip tightened and her sweet smile melted away. "Once they walk through that door, the demons enchant them to remain. We learned that we can use the animals to keep other witches away. Can you believe our luck, Fredda? Our dear sister brought us exactly what we needed. A wolf strong enough to help us."

"*Yes, you did…*" the serpent demon intoned to her. "*Bring the animals to come play with us.*"

ACCORDING TO YOLANDE, THE BREACH OCCURRED NOT far from where she'd spoken to Brian and Zach yesterday.

This early in the evening, the sky was clear, but a hint of fog covered the ground as they hiked uphill.

The wolves were getting closer to the position.

"No sound," Zach said.

Brian and Janet nodded.

At least his cohorts for this mission had dressed properly. Janet now wore a pair of dark trousers and boots from the witches, while Brian had donned jeans he'd borrowed from Zach.

They crept forward, listening for any sounds. They had to be close. The wolf within Zach stirred to life. He hungered for an all-out fight, but he only had an inkling of what they'd face.

He motioned for Brian and Janet to spread out. A single hit from a projectile could take out all of them at once.

Then a new scent crossed his nose. Two women. They'd come from a metropolitan area. Pollution and perfume clung to their clothes. Could the witches detect them or approach like Yolande had snuck up on them?

He put up his hand and gave the signal to indicate two targets ahead. Janet nodded, while Brian appeared puzzled.

Not good.

Janet mouthed, "Two people. Be careful."

Finally, Brian got the gist and gave a thumbs-up.

They drew closer. The hooting barred owls went silent. The wind whistling through the trees was the only sound.

He crept forward until a high-pitched sound sliced through him. Not far from him, the other werewolves cringed.

Shit, did the attackers know they faced werewolves? There went the element of surprise. Brian was the first to bolt away toward the source.

"No," Zach said. "It's a trap."

Zach sprinted after him. Low-lying branches smacked his cheek and the uneven terrain slowed him down, but he picked up speed.

He could spot Brian ahead of him. Janet wasn't far behind, but she kept her distance. The roar of the ocean drifted to him. How close were they to the high cliffs?

Closer and closer. He pumped his legs until he reached out and snatched the back of Brian's collar.

Right before Brian slipped off the edge of a cliff face to the black water below.

"Oh, fuck me," Brian said, gasping.

The shrill noise still persisted and created an ache in the back of Zach's head.

If their targets had the power of illusion to create the sound and mess with their eyes, what could he use to find them?

From the gear strapped to his shoulder, he snagged his FLIR PVS-7 night-vision goggles. He quickly scanned the rocky hills. The trees obscured many places, but their targets couldn't completely hide.

The thermal imaging in the goggles revealed two figures perched behind trees about a hundred yards away.

Zach pointed and crouched. "There, past the birch trees. Right next to that pine that's about to fall over."

Brian grimaced from the harsh sound but confirmed he'd sighted them.

"Go north. Redirect their attention to you."

"Why?"

Now wasn't the time for questions. "We can't hit them head-on." He added a *push* to his words. "We *have* to work together or they will attack the coven. If they get past us, they'll take Lark."

Brian's features darkened with displeasure at being ordered around, but he nodded and slipped out of his clothes.

Zach didn't wait to witness the transformation. He didn't need a reminder of how painful getting your bones and insides rearranged could be.

Once Brian sprinted off, Zach darted from tree to tree until he reached Janet's position. He relayed the plan, and she ran south.

Good.

Briefly, he winced. The noise's intensity magnified, scratching and clawing at his skull, but he wasn't far from them now. Fifty feet. Twenty-five feet. He could faintly make out their backs through the fog. Hear their heartbeats. Smell the heavy scent of copper in the air.

They feared him, but they were ready to use their blood magic.

With ease, he could be on them and they'd succumb with a few hits.

Suddenly, a dark wolf emerged from the brush, its mouth open wide and claws extended.

One of the witches screamed while the other extended a bloody hand in Brian's direction. In one moment, Brian was in midair, ready to plow into the first witch; in the next, a great whoosh propelled him upward to the trees.

Fuck. They might be dead meat.

Abandoning the element of surprise, Zach jumped onto the leaning pine, then launched himself in their direction. He landed hard and rolled to stand before the first witch. Using an open-palm strike, he struck her at half strength in her solar plexus. The witch bowed inward and fell to her feet.

He prepared to twist and face the other witch—right as an unseen force smacked his ribs. *Crack. Crack.* The witch's magic threw him into the brush, where he landed on his back.

The blow sucked the air from his lungs, and the immediate pain to his stomach caught him off guard.

Get up, McGinnis. You're not dead meat yet.

He staggered to his feet to see Janet rush in from the front while Brian came at them from the back.

Utter chaos.

He waited for the blood witch to kill them, but Janet pounced on her first, followed by Brian. The witch's startled screams ended abruptly.

Zach hurried to subdue the other witch, but Brian switched targets and sank his teeth into the fallen assassin.

"No!" Zach barked.

But it was too late.

The fog stirred and the barred owls resumed their calling. And now two people were dead and could no longer answer questions.

Fury and frustration pulsed through him. He waited for

Janet and Brian to revert to their human forms before he spoke again.

"What did you do?" Zach asked slowly.

"I took care of them," Brian said firmly.

Zach's jaw twitched with irritation. "They were more valuable to us alive than dead."

"So they can do more of that magic shit against us?" Brian sneered as he got dressed. "I'll pass."

Janet's head hung low and she gave Zach a look of empathy.

"They could have told us where to find Justine. She has to have a base of operations somewhere on the mainland."

Brian snorted. "When the next ones show up, you can invite them over and chat if you want. The way I see it, we have higher odds of survival against these *magicians* if we kill them first and ask questions later."

Kill first. Plan later. Was that what they'd taught him as a risk analyst?

Zach used to think that way before his time as a hunter, but time and experience had taught him there'd be consequences for such actions. Without a chain of command, a party of hunters had a higher chance of leaving a wolf's den in body bags versus their own two feet.

If he wanted to protect Lark, he had to check Brian, and soon—or the body bags would start piling up on their side.

~

HEARING THE TATTOO'S VOICE ALWAYS RATTLED HER. SHE half expected the women around her to react, but no one ever did.

Having self-deprecating doubts was natural, but the demon's voice made it all too real. Something lived inside of her.

And it had no intention of leaving.

"And what if I don't want to bring them to you?" Lark whispered fiercely to Fredda.

Fredda pursed her lips. "You don't have to deliver them to us. We'll simply *take* them. If necessary, for the coven's safety," she added.

"Those people you call animals have free will—" Lark began.

Zenobia slapped her cheek. "Shut up, willful witch!"

The sting left Lark wide-eyed and stunned.

On her belly, the coiled serpent stretched out and *flexed*. An unseen force shoved the two blood witches back a couple of steps.

Zenobia smirked and discarded her shawl, revealing the sleeveless blouse she wore. "It's *awake*. Good. We may need it."

Lark gaped upon seeing the mysterious tattoo she'd only glimpsed before. The writhing tentacles from a great squid stretched down Zenobia's arms.

Suddenly, a commotion erupted upstairs. The sounds of heavy footsteps and objects hit the wooden floor overhead.

Zenobia sighed. "That didn't take long."

"Long for what?" Lark followed Fredda up the ladder to the hidden room. Once she'd climbed up to the next floor, she noticed the door had been shut and reinforced with metal planks from their side.

A heavy object slammed against the door. Dust fell along the door's seams. The metal plank groaned.

"What's going on out there?" Lark whispered.

"The box is calling a witch," Fredda said. "I'll silence the house."

Zenobia tugged Lark back to the ladder. "There is nothing we can do but repair their prison while Fredda protects us. Their call will be weakened if we're successful."

Lark nearly fell down the ladder, but the old woman jerked her along.

"But *what's* attacking the door?"

Zenobia mumbled words in Latin—which turned to English. *"We bind you in light. We bind you in blood."*

Then she turned to Lark. "It's not a *what*. It's a who. The demons in the box have called our sisters to them." She pointed to a spot on the other side of the pedestal in the center of the room. "Stand here and concentrate."

More objects rattled above them. Almost as if they were being hurled into every heavy piece of furniture at the doorway.

Or maybe the slams came from *prying* it open.

"Repeat after me." Zenobia repeated the incantation in Latin.

Lark couldn't follow along with the foreign words, so she said the spell in English. "We bind you in light. We bind you in blood."

While Lark spoke, Zenobia reached into the weathered open box in the corner and plucked out what appeared to be an antique cigar box. She lifted the lid and removed a set of rotten cigars, unbothered by the chaos above their heads.

Would Lark survive to defend the box if the blood witches stormed inside?

What if it wasn't a woman attacking them, but a child?

Her breath came out in gasps, but she kept speaking.

As Zenobia placed the now-empty cigar box next to the demon's fractured home, Lark caught the sounds of the metal plank on the door upstairs giving way.

The ladder fell to the floor. Lark's gaze connected with Fredda's determined one before the wooden hatch was slammed shut.

"Keep talking!" Zenobia barked.

Lark snapped her attention back to the side-by-side

boxes. She watched Zenobia place the smaller box inside of the cigar box.

"We bind you in light. We bind you in blood," Zenobia whispered. Her pleas picked up speed as someone—no more than one person—fought above them. A woman screamed. Then another—their cries silenced with wet groans.

Zenobia's spell came at a frantic pace. Lark gripped the pedestal. A sheen of sweat dampened her forehead.

They will not open the door. They will not open that damn door.

Her heart beat so fast that she could taste her pulse. The words she spoke bled together.

Over and over again until Zenobia slumped to the floor.

"Zenobia!" Lark hurried over to the fallen woman.

Zenobia's breath was shallow and her pulse slow, but she was alive. Did she need medical attention?

Lark glanced at the hatch.

A deathly silence filled the small room. Nothing stirred above them.

Had Fredda survived?

Minutes passed. Then the hatch swung open and Fredda appeared.

Lark gasped.

Splotches of blood covered Fredda's face. Even more blood dripped from along the edge of the hatch into the room below. A fingernail fell from above. Horrified, Lark scooted back.

What the hell happened up there?

Voice empty, Fredda said, "The box is fixed. Bring me the ladder."

When Lark didn't move fast enough, Fredda said, "Wake up, Lark. Ladder, please."

Hands shaking, Lark scrambled to put the ladder in

place. Fredda climbed down, nodded with approval at the box, and checked on Zenobia.

Lark's back hit the cold stone wall.

Right in front of her, Fredda's clothes were covered in bloody matter. Fear washed over Lark again as a thought bubbled: what powers did Fredda's tattoo grant her?

And what had she done to protect this room?

Lark had to see. She had to know if her aunt, Yolande, or anyone else she had come to know hadn't survived. She hurried up the ladder and slowly peeked over the edge.

Bodies everywhere.

Or maybe she was seeing two to three people hacked to pieces.

The door hung off its hinges. Broken furniture was scattered across the great room beyond this one.

Then a foul smell smacked her face. It was the dead. The copper-heavy scent seeped into her pores. Bile shot up the back of her throat. She covered her mouth. She refused to vomit here.

Opening and closing her shaking hands couldn't stop the numb feeling washing over her.

Get the hell out of here. Don't look at this anymore, she thought.

She tried to find a clean place to step, but every surface was soiled.

Death reigned here.

As she escaped, the snake slid back and forth along her spine.

It was joyous. That evil *thing* reveled in absolute bliss as her disgust deepened.

[16]

CLOUDS FROM AN ONCOMING SNOWSTORM OBSCURED the morning sun. The breeze off the coast whipped against Lark's face, but she didn't feel it.

The morning cold will make it go away, she prayed.

Two blood witches had died. Yolande was wounded, but she'd survive.

And the ceremony was complete. Finally.

Lark had witnessed it all as the long night passed, but the numbness she carried after leaving the house persisted.

The morning cold must make the madness go away.

But the circumstances hadn't changed: the witches wanted her to give them one of her friends—in particular, Zach.

She left the Mountain Haven House to see Zach returning from the woods.

Damn you, Z. Your loyalty to me will get you killed one day.

Instead of walking up to him, she hurried around the main house until she stood in front of the fence where the yard ended, and jagged rocks leading to the Pacific loomed below.

"You want to talk about it?" Zach joined her at the fence.

"Is the border secure?" she asked.

The weight of his gaze nearly suffocated her. "Justine sent two blood witches and we handled them. I also put in trip-wires in addition to their wards. We're safe. For now."

He'd fought on her behalf, waited for her all night, and she couldn't face him. Every time she closed her eyes, the ceremony flashed before her eyes.

What a fool she'd been to believe this would all be so simple.

"Ready to talk?" he asked.

Her chest grew tight until she steadied herself. "Not yet. I'm still trying to…" She searched for the right word, but she couldn't find it.

"You're trying to process everything."

"Yeah." Process how to get Zach the fuck out of here.

The gusts of wind chilled her skin. She shivered, hoping for clarity, but none came.

The blood. Why did there have to be so much blood last night?

Zach gathered her into his arms, pressing her back to him. Her eyes fluttered shut as serenity tried to take over.

No, you have work to do, she reminded herself. *Don't get attached.*

She returned to the Lake House, and Zach followed. "Remember when I said I wanted answers?" she asked.

"Of course." His wider stride helped him catch up to walk beside her.

"I regret it now."

"Did they hurt you? What happened last night?" He circled in front of her to block her path.

"No, it's not like that." The intensity in his eyes made it hard for her to look at him, but she forced herself to accept this new side of him. "Matter of fact, Zenobia and Fredda fear the snake demon I carry. So far it's protected me from harm, but someday they believe I will be coerced to use it against others. Like Folake."

"And what do you *regret*?"

She snorted. "'Be careful what you wish for' would be the best way to put it."

She'd wanted too much: knowledge, understanding, and direction when she didn't have any after Dad died.

She sucked in a deep breath to prepare herself for what had to be said. "You need to take my guardians and leave."

His steadfast expression never faltered. "Are you serious?"

"I wish I was. The madness last night was well deserved. A demon box is nothing to be fucked with—the things trapped inside the box call to blood witches to set them free." The carnage flashed through her mind, and she winced. "For centuries, the witches have used werewolves to guard the demons' prisons."

"So that's why we're *animals*. Can't have your guard dogs be seen as humans."

"It's more than that. Power corrupts, and it's evident here. The blood witches are as elitist as hell. Younger witches go out into the world and enslave werewolves. Those men and women, in turn, are compelled to go to the room with the box, and they *never* return." She shook her head with disgust at the implications. "A rogue here or there wouldn't be missed. My dad never mentioned them, but I can imagine he'd help the witches if that meant there'd be one less were-wolf killing innocent people."

"That belief is a myth."

"I know that now. Which is why you three need to escape while you still can."

"No," he said firmly.

"This isn't a game, Z."

"Staying here never was a game. It's *life*. The stage is set.

You accept the change in players, the unanticipated moves, and you make decisions to win." He reached out and stroked her cheek.

Reluctantly, she leaned into his hand. "They will imprison you. If not you, then Janet or Brian."

Don't make me force you to leave, you stubborn bastard.

"No." He didn't budge. "No more running. We're stronger together."

Did he mean everyone—or just them?

She searched his face. Ran her fingertip along the stubble on his chin, then up the curve of his cheek. Zach's nostrils flared, and she marveled at the effect she still had on him.

Did he still want her?

He slipped an arm around her waist and pulled her closer to him. Close enough for his body to block the wind, yet for her to feel every hard inch of him.

"I want to be strong," she murmured, wanting to add "for you," but she couldn't.

He kissed her forehead then the tip of her nose. "You already are." His warm breath fanned her face. They shared an exhale before his nose brushed hers and he claimed her mouth.

Kissing Zachary McGinnis was an experience. He tended to be a nibbler, tracing a line of heat from her mouth down to her neck—the ultimate target for hickeys—but this time she wasn't ready for such a deep kiss, an embrace that weakened her knees and left her hungry as they parted.

She gave a soft laugh. "You've upped your game, Z."

He rolled his eyes and snuck in another breathtaking kiss. "I haven't changed. You're still the last woman I kissed."

Her face grew warm as she grinned. "Not a ladies' man anymore?"

He gave her the mischievous grin she'd missed. "I've been a bit busy lately."

"Excuses. Excuses."

He sighed, and she did the same.

"What now?" she asked. "The problem remains."

"Yes, it does."

"I still want us to leave."

"Then the tattoo will compel you to *kill* everyone in every hiding place you seek," he said with absolute seriousness.

"What are you saying?"

"Yolande told me everything." He relayed the reason Justine wanted her dead. How the woman believed killing Lark would set all the witches free and why Lark stood a better chance if she stayed with the Painted Coven. "Yolande told me Justine is capable of catastrophic destruction."

She cursed. God help her, she was screwed unless she got them all to leave her behind. "We'll talk more inside. You're turning into a Popsicle."

Snow began to fall as they walked hand in hand to the Lake House. Janet and Brian glanced up from where they sat at the kitchenette table. At least they were alive.

For now.

"We were worried about you," Janet said with a small smile, "but it looks like Zach has things covered."

Zach pulled out a chair for her. Instead of sitting, she leaned against it. A yawn snuck up on her. Sleep was out of the question too. The last thing she wanted was to have a nightmare about the last twenty-four hours.

It wasn't the time to rest yet, either.

"We need a plan, everyone," she said.

Janet placed a cup of tea on the table. "What's up?"

Lark took a long drink. "If you'd seen what I saw last night, we'd all be strapping ourselves into straitjackets." She told Janet and Brian about the witches' plans. "Sooner or later, they'll come for you. I'll try to stop them, but we need to be ready for anything at this point. I regret bringing you both into this." Exhaustion and frustration hit her. A hot tear slipped down her cheek. She wiped it away and straightened her back.

"Tears never solved problems," Mom used to say. As a kid, Lark *hated* that saying. Sometimes crying helped, but not today. They needed a plan to keep everyone save until she figured out how to deal with Justine.

Speaking of the bitch she'd never met… "Do they know about Justine?"

"Brian knows," Zach replied.

"He already told me," Janet added.

"And none of you thought I should know what Justine is capable of doing?" Lark said as Janet poured more tea for her.

"Sit down and stop trying to save the world." Janet gently pushed against Lark's shoulders until she sat in the nearest seat.

That made her almost laugh. Hadn't she said the same thing to Z?

"We didn't say anything since we knew you'd find out soon enough," Brian said with a shrug.

Lark laughed. There wasn't much else she could do. "I could use some good news for once."

Janet searched through the cabinets. She was quite the master at getting past the child-safe locks. Once she found what she was looking for, she returned to Lark and added a shot of vodka to the tea.

"That's not exactly a *healthy* choice," Lark said.

Janet winked at her. "We'll pretend it's water."

Lark glanced at the bottle and snorted. Now why did the caregivers have a liquor stash in the house? Guess everyone needed refreshments every now and then.

"Can I have some?" Brian asked. "Since everyone is having some medicine."

"You can have more water," Janet replied drily. "Zach, you want some?"

Zach snagged a glass of tap water. "Naw, I'll drink water with Brian."

"Don't bother. It doesn't taste very good," Brian mumbled.

They all laughed.

It felt good for Lark to forget about her troubles briefly. She'd face them again soon enough.

EVENING CREPT IN, BRINGING FRIGID TEMPERATURES and a stillness back to the grounds. Snow continued to fall and pile up on the deck shrubbery and plants. Lark hurried to the Lake House. She had much to do before dinner began at seven.

She'd left the house after Zach had fallen asleep on the living room couch, but she didn't expect him to sleep for long. Exhaustion clung to them both after the events today, but Lark wouldn't be able to rest until she knew what to do in the coming days.

One of the witchlings working in the kitchen directed her to Fredda's quarters. She trailed after the small girl, neither of them speaking.

Lark sighed, looking at the child's small back. The little girl reminded her of her cousin's daughter Tia. The demon box's arrival wasn't Lark's fault, but Justine's continued attack would be on her hands.

Whether she could face Justine alone or not, it was up to her to bring this fight elsewhere.

Down the hallway Lark took the other day to reach Iluminada's room, the girl led her to a door near the staircase.

"Here," the girl said.

"Thanks."

The girl hurried to escape down the steps, stopped, then whispered, "You're welcome."

Lark knocked a couple of times. First softly, then harder.

"You needed me?" Fredda's voice came from behind her.

Lark turned. "Oh, sorry. I thought you were in there." She peeked around Fredda. How had she snuck up so quietly? "I came for help."

Fredda crossed her arms. "I wondered how long it would take you to show up." Amusement shone in her dark eyes.

"I was going to ask Zenobia to teach me a thing or two about my tattoo, but she's a bit rough around the edges."

"Don't I know it. She hasn't changed and grows more crotchety over time."

"After what happened last night, I need to be ready to defend myself against Justine. And I have no idea where to start."

Fredda's face softened, and she reached out to pat Lark's shoulder. The bracelets on her wrist jingled. "We could start with the obvious—don't fight her at all."

"I think I'm past that point. I wish I could hide away."

Fredda chuckled. "Got any spare nuclear bunkers?"

"Oh, stop it, I'm serious."

"That bitch is crazy. Iluminada has told me some wild tales about growing up with Jussie. I know enough to never cross her. I've only witnessed the smear marks of the people she wiped off the face of the Earth. What are you thinking of doing?"

"I need to know how to use the serpent before it uses me. Especially if the coven needs the wolves."

Fredda sighed. "If we don't get them from you, we will find them elsewhere."

"Do you even hear what you're saying, Fredda? Those people are my friends."

"And I'm talking about preventing mankind's extinction." She tilted her head and her gaze hardened. "No, the ends do not justify the means, but you need to wake up. Understand *our* stakes before you judge the sisterhood."

The patter of footsteps at the bottom of the stairwell silenced the both of them. Once they knew the witchling had passed, Freda continued. "I don't mean to be so hard on you." She sighed. "I've stood on the frontlines for so long that the lines between what's right and wrong have blurred."

Lark nodded. Fredda didn't look her age—not a single wrinkle marred the blemish-free skin on her face.

But Fredda's dark eyes spoke a different tale. A tale of sorry and wisdom hard-earned, of loss and time.

"We'll get started tonight after dinner," Fredda said firmly. "Go get some rest and eat dinner early. Jussie sent the first wave last night, so we have some time before she attacks again."

[17]

AROUND SEVEN A.M., ZACH STIRRED TO WAKE UP AFTER a well-deserved sleep. He wasn't alone in the queen-sized bed —Lark faced him fast asleep.

She could've stayed in another room to add distance between them, but why had she chosen to stay here? He shifted to slip out of the bed. Lark's hand latched onto his arm. Her eyes opened briefly.

"I want you to stay," she whispered. "With me."

He smiled and drew her into his arms. There wasn't much space on the bed in the caregiver's private room, but they'd made it work. She snuggled against his shoulder and drifted off again.

Briefly, he listened for any suspicious sounds. Nothing was amiss. Over the night, nothing had stirred and he'd managed to rest.

He twisted a bit, finding his cracked ribs less painful. Very nice.

He could get used to this rapid-healing thing.

Back when he was a hunter, he would've spent weeks in bed to stabilize his torso. Add to that hours with ice packs and doing *anything* to prevent himself from sneezing or coughing.

Even the memory of the horrific pain made him wince.

Now he was free to do what needed to be done: protect Lark.

No more running for either of them. He nuzzled her neck, then slipped his right hand underneath her shirt to slide his palm against her smooth, warm skin.

He glanced down to see her staring right back at him.

"I'm going to kiss you, Captain Killjoy," she whispered.

LARK KISSED HIS NOSE.

Zach McGinnis was still trying to save the world. Could she save him from himself? Just the very idea of seeing him trapped in that room made her heart ache, but she didn't want to let him go.

"Hello, beautiful," he murmured.

His hand drifted upward, brushing against the underside of her breast. His fingertips caressed her nipple before he rested his palm against her chest. Right where her heart lay. Suddenly, honeyed warmth enveloped her. Breathtaking pleasure coursed from her stomach and spread down into her legs. When the pleasurable feeling surged to her core, she moaned softly.

"Mmm," she whispered. "That's you, isn't it?"

He nodded, his hazel eyes stormy and feral as he leaned over her. Hovering. Waiting to kiss her lips. How she'd missed the anticipation.

Briefly, he brushed his upper lip against her lower one. Sparks lit a path across her skin. His first kiss was tentative—but then again, wasn't their first time together the same?

He kissed her again, and they tilted their heads to settle

into a familiar rhythm. Into a deep kiss where her breath caught. Then his tongue darted against hers. Delight danced down her spine. They were close, but they could be much closer. She shifted a bit. Now his arousal pressed against her thigh. If she angled her hips just right, she could truly feel him. She moved. Now he rested between her legs.

He's exactly *where I want him.*

She rocked her hips, back and forth, upward and downward, rubbing her core along the length straining in his pants.

Zach groaned with pleasure and caressed her shoulders. From there, he lightly ran his fingertips against her waist and hips. "I can't tell you how much I've wanted to touch you again."

Before she could reply, he helped her out of her T-shirt and bra. Then his mouth was on her bare breasts. He nibbled along every curve. Every sensitive spot.

Still a nibbler, she thought with a sigh.

"You smell so good." He flicked his tongue from one mocha-brown areola to another. "I couldn't wait to taste you."

"I'm not stopping you…"

The morning light seeping through the thick curtains muted her view, but she could make out the top of his head as he sucked and nibbled his way downward. She reached for him, but he grabbed her arms and held them above her head.

"Stay." His voice was hoarse and thick.

Damn, she found that sexy.

She wanted to touch him and grip his thick hair, anything to distract herself from the building pleasure.

He gave her a devilish grin before he sucked hard at one nipple then shifted to slowly lick the other.

That's definitely a new move, Mr. McGinnis, she thought.

Suddenly, his hands were at her hips, unbuttoning her

pants and tugging them down. She lifted her hips to help him.

"Zach…we don't have any protection," she whispered.

"We don't need it anymore."

"Huh?"

"I learned it's different for werewolves. I choose when to…you know, make you pregnant."

"Oh." She chuckled a bit then reached for him again. Tentatively, she drew his shirt off him. Her hands roamed over his chest, eliciting a moan from him as her hands brushed against his nipples. He was a beautiful specimen. She counted one, two, three lines of muscle long his quivering stomach.

She wanted to trace her tongue over each of them.

A red mark drew her eye to his chest. His hunter tattoo was inked on his left pec. She traced her fingers over the red paw print. The serpent drifted along her lower back while she circled his nipple with her fingertip.

Now, that *part hasn't changed either,* she thought with a sly grin.

Once he was naked, he tugged one of her legs over his shoulders.

"Z." The moment his mouth brushed against her core, her legs trembled.

"I told you I couldn't wait." With one long lick, he fired every nerve ending between her legs.

She gasped and swallowed a curse.

Zach McGinnis had improved in more ways than one. He stroked her with his tongue, sampling every part of her. She screamed his name again and again as a climax swept over her. By the time she released her tight grip on his hair, he wrapped her legs around his hips, and then his hard length was inside her.

Yes, she'd missed this feeling. She could forget about the

outside world and only exist with him. Feel him inside her. Touching her. Kissing her.

Still nibbling on her. But she didn't mind that.

In the past, he'd always let her set the pace. Sometimes, he'd finished first during quickies. Other times, she did.

This time was different. The changes were subtle, from the quickening of his hips as he thrust, to the hardening grip of his hands on her buttocks as he thrust deep. Her back arched.

"So sweet," he growled.

Their gazes connected, and she fell into his eyes. They resembled molten gold. She felt the same way. Scorching. She burned for more.

He kissed her again, and she surrendered, gripping his back and waiting for the release to come. The buildup was there and she fell over the edge.

[18]

Two quiet days passed. Snow accumulated on the trees, dusting the tall pine and cedars with fine snowflakes.

Spending his nights in Lark's arms steadied Zach for the conflicts to come. As he stood guard on the edge of the forest overlooking the houses, he grinned like a fool, recalling how she'd kept pulling him back to bed.

Not for sex, but to sleep a bit longer.

He laughed and rested against a tree, waiting for Lark to finish training with Fredda and see her safely back to Lake House.

Even with all the dangers here, this place had been good for them. Not that this was a safe haven by any means, but they had moments to connect, to talk about the past.

He spied a figure near the edge of Lake House walking toward the main house. Janet stiffly made her way there. She didn't have a coat on—not that she needed it, but it wasn't like Janet to leave the house unless she had a purpose.

What was she doing?

He took a step forward.

Janet kept ambling toward Mountain Haven House,

165

stumbling over an urn on the back deck. She got to her feet and kept going.

She didn't even bother to remove the snow caking her side.

Shit.

Zach broke into a hard run. Janet reached the side of the house and bumped into landscaping. Yolande emerged from the back door.

Just as Yolande thundered down the back steps toward Janet, Zach jumped in front of the guardian.

"Stop," he commanded.

Janet came to a halt. She looked up at him, mouth wide. "What…am I doing here?"

He gently grabbed her shoulders. "It's not safe for you here."

This place was deadly in more ways than one. At first, the blood demon's prison had been a subtle pull, stretching at least ten yards away from the house, but now the call's strength had increased. He could feel it too, tugging and clawing at him to storm his way into the house.

"Return to the Lake House," he said. "Keep away from the main house until further notice."

"But what if Lark——"

"I'll wait for her training to end today."

He waited for clarity to return to her eyes before he released her.

Janet sighed and retreated a step before pausing. "Thanks, Zach."

"No problem."

"There's something you should know." She looked away. "Brian is still upset, and he's hiding something from me. I don't know what—but you should be careful."

~

THE INVITE TO DROP BY THE GOSSAMER HOUSE LATER that evening caught Lark off guard.

"Are you sure one of the caregivers asked me to come over?" she asked Janet as they approached the red house's back door.

"Oh, stop it," Janet chided her. "I promise I didn't tell them about your third head. Or your tendency to drool when you sleep."

Lark snorted. "It's always about the first impression, isn't it?"

They didn't have to wait long outside the door. A woman Lark learned was named Avril beckoned them inside with a grin.

"Right on time!" she said brightly. "The kids were about to raid the popcorn."

Lark stumbled across the threshold, and Janet tugged her forward.

"Are you sure they want me here?" Lark whispered. "I'm public enemy number one."

Janet rolled her eyes and pushed her glasses up.

Lark followed her guardian through the maze of shoes and boots on the floors. Dark wool coats were crammed in every corner. All the children's belongings from the Lake House had migrated here. The sweet smell of caramel popcorn drifted around the corner.

The mudroom led to a small kitchen. Much smaller than the Lake House. How had they managed? Lark recalled seeing at least a dozen girls when they'd first arrived.

Girlish chatter and conversation emerged from the living room. They followed the sounds until they reached a packed room. Girls filled every space, many of them with blankets and bowls of popcorn. To Lark's delight, several younger girls sipped a pink concoction through straws.

Wow, they even have milkshakes, she thought. They knew

how to throw a movie party. The television on the other side of the room was paused on the opening credits to Disney's *Cinderella*. A classic, if anyone asked Lark.

"Hurry up," one little dark-haired girl declared.

Lark wasn't sure where to sit until two teenage witchlings got up and motioned for Lark and Janet to sit on the couch.

"We can stand in the back," Lark said softly.

"Elders sit there." Before she could protest, the girls ushered them to the open spots. Even more surprising, one of the younger witchlings got up and sat in Janet's lap.

"Hey, my sweet girl," Janet murmured to the child.

"Well, hello there." Lark tried not to smile like a fool.

What had changed? Apparently, she was no longer a threat. As she surveyed the room of young faces, warmth filled her chest.

"It seems like you've been over here before," Lark whispered.

"Two of the caregivers are pregnant," Janet explained.

That made Lark chortle. The sharp-eyed midwife had made herself useful.

Then the movie started. The opening music's horns and the soft voices eased the tension in Lark's shoulders. A cheesy grin broke out on her face. Like any night owl as a child, she'd watched these films with her mom, and now she got to experience a happily-ever-after with the younger witches.

Perhaps she shouldn't have judged the Painted Coven so harshly.

[19]

THE NEXT MORNING, LARK GOT UP BEFORE THE SUN rose. Tendrils of light peeked along the closed curtains, but darkness prevailed.

Zach's heavy arm was draped over her waist, but she slipped off the bed without waking him up.

Captain Killjoy needs his rest, she thought.

She got dressed into a sweater and jeans, then she hurried out of the room. To her surprise, she passed Janet in the kitchen giving one of the pregnant witches a checkup.

"You heading out?" Janet asked.

The blood witch glanced at Lark, not with concern, but a casual wave.

"I'm meeting Fredda for a lesson." Lark donned her coat. "Don't worry. We're probably going to sit around and talk for a while."

Thirty minutes later, all that gossiping Lark thought she'd experience hadn't panned out.

"You're not focusing." Fredda gave Lark an annoyed look again.

"Sorry." Lark shifted in her cushioned seat and tried to

concentrate.

The pair sat face to face in a well-lit alcove in Fredda's private quarters. It was difficult not to doze off in the elder blood witch's room. The serene sky-blue walls made Lark want to drift away, while sapphire-blue silk curtains surrounding the windows invited her to touch them. Fredda had decorated her room in a manner similar to Iluminada, with a comfortable sitting area with vermillion sofa and lush silk pillows on the floor. Antique urns and pitchers added a rustic touch to the room.

But it was the thin cloud of incense, with the rich scent of peppermint, that relaxed Lark the most.

Based on the stern look on Fredda's face, she wouldn't have a great shot at borrowing any.

"I just don't feel anything happening," she admitted. "The damn thing moves when *it* wants to move."

Fredda sighed. "Let's take a break for a little while, then."

"I don't think a break will help much, but sure." Lark relaxed in the seat, and her gaze drifted to the window. "It's so beautiful outside. Were you born here?"

"Oh no, I used to live in the U.S. with the Cardinal Coven in Massachusetts." Fredda's expression grew wistful. "When I was around ten, things went sour when a demon escaped the box the coven guarded."

"Damn."

"Yeah, the sisters fought it down to the last woman, but even she didn't survive after she contained it."

"What happened to you?"

She sighed, and Lark watched the wave of emotions—sadness, grief—wash over her face as the tendrils of incense floated upward. "This was back in 1930s, so back then Black children like me weren't treated well. The authorities scattered most of the white witches to orphanages across the state while I ended up with Miss Contessa Galveston." She harrumphed. "She was a social worker, and I use that word loosely. That woman didn't want a child to raise. She wanted a servant. From the start of the day to the end, she expected me to clean and cook."

"I'm sorry," Lark said softly.

"One of my earliest memories was Contessa scurrying me around the house to pick up after one of her *suitors* came over. Those heathens left dirty clothes, crushed cigarette butts, and food everywhere." She grimaced as if she smelled something foul. "I had to eat their leftovers, if I ever found any."

"How did you get away? Didn't you know magic?"

"I was a witchling that had grown up in an isolated home. I didn't know anything about the outside world or the dangers it held." She gave Lark a long look. "I lived in that horrible house until Zenobia found me."

Outside the window, the wind rustled the trees. Lark briefly imagined another house in Massachusetts where a young Fredda was trapped with no safe place to go.

She offered Lark a hopeful smile. "Many other things have happened to me—I won't go into them right now—but now I'm here and I have *purpose*. You'll find your purpose, too."

Fredda reached out for Lark's hand.

Lark offered it.

"Let's get back to business." Fredda glanced at Lark's right hand as if to examine it—before whacking the top good. Not once, but twice.

"Ow!" Pain surged up Lark's arm. A second later, the serpent demon stirred from its position around her stomach. "That's weird. It moved."

"I was hoping to avoid using this method, but the 'concentrate and meditate' method ain't for you."

"True. Why do people learn to concentrate anyway?"

"I need you to learn how to hyper-focus, if possible, but for now you're going to have to live in the trenches." Fredda crossed her legs and drew her black cotton skirt up to her knees.

"Nice legs," Lark remarked.

"Oh, stop." Fredda chuckled. "Just wait."

A sliver of a vibrant periwinkle feather peeked from under the dress on Fredda's right knee. The feather elongated, traveling downward until Lark could make out the telltale eyelike tips of a peacock's feathers.

"A bird," she whispered.

"A very chatty little bitch," Fredda said. "But all those years living with Mrs. Galveston and her men gave me plenty of food to feed her. Now I get what I *want* in return."

Fredda grabbed a bloodletting box from a stone end table next to the chairs. From inside she withdrew a needle.

"Why do you need that?" Lark asked.

"Wait." Fredda pricked the sensitive skin between her left hand's thumb and index finger. Nothing happened until she pressed the needle in deep. She hissed from the pain—right as the feathers fluttered.

With her teeth clenched, Fredda said, "The demon is usually sleeping, but it can be awakened with the right pain and suffering, whether it's mental or physical. Got it?"

With intensity, she added, "Your true goal is to find deep *anguish*." She inhaled deeply and, before Lark's very eyes, Fredda shimmered in the light.

Her black braided hair shortened. Black fur sprouted on her skin as her face elongated into a wolf's jaw. Her hand, which had once clenched the needle, turned into a paw with sharp claws.

Seconds later, Fredda fell to the floor with a heavy thud.

Lark scrambled backward, not believing her eyes.

Laughter filled the corner. One second the werewolf

stood there, ready to pounce, and in the next, Lark found laughing Fredda still sitting in the chair.

"That wasn't funny," Lark said, her voice a bit shaky.

"No, it wasn't, but I don't get to play that trick often."

"Did you really change into a werewolf?" If so, Fredda's powers were pretty badass.

"The peacock demon is a master of illusions. As a defensive measure, people automatically see what they fear the most." She sucked in a breath. "When I wield my demon, others see what *I* want them to see. And the outcome is always far more frightening than what you witnessed."

Lark settled back into the seat and leaned forward. "So when you had to keep those witches away from the box…"

Fredda had a faraway look in her eyes. "I gave them horrific visions until they went mad and ripped each other apart."

She sighed, and soon enough, the jovial Fredda returned. "It's your turn now." She plucked another needle from the box and offered it to Lark.

"But I've already learned how to prick myself. Do I have to stab the shit out of myself to make progress?"

Fredda pursed her lips. "You got a better idea?"

"Not yet," Lark admitted.

She eyed the end of the needle. Of course, the witch had handed her a bigger one than the minuscule one Fredda used to prick her finger. Lark ran the fingertip of her left index finger over the point. Nice and sharp. She took aim.

She stared at the skin between her index finger and thumb, imagining the pain. This wouldn't be pretty…

"You need me to demonstrate again?" Fredda asked.

Lark shuddered. "I'll pass. I almost climbed your walls there." She blew out a deep breath and got into position again to do the deed.

Fredda folded her arms.

Each time Lark prepared to strike, she hesitated. Instead of thinking about the needle, she set her attention on her target.

Make it quick. Get it done.

She blew out a breath and brought the needle down hard. Pain exploded from her hand—and the snake coiled, tightening along her torso and rearing as if to open its great mouth and swallow everything whole.

With the next inhale, Lark shuddered as the snake released its grip. A second later, the window next to them crumbled inward as if a giant's hand had ripped the window from the sill.

Snowflakes floated into the room to join glass scattered over the floor.

Good God, did I do that?

She gaped at the aftermath, slowly turning her head to Fredda. "Guess we won't be practicing in here anymore."

NOT LONG AFTER COVERING UP THE JAGGED OPENING IN Fredda's room, Lark returned to the Lake House. Her thoughts were scattered, but her sense of purpose strengthened.

Using the serpent demon was a last resort, but not knowing how to use it wasn't wise.

She entered the house to find Brian and Zach preparing weapons.

"What's going on?" She surveyed the table to find four Sig Sauer P320s, two Heckler & Koch P30Ls, a lovely sniper rifle, and tactical gear. "Are we going to war?"

"Pretty much." Brian sat off to the side, looking out of place while Zach loaded the P320s.

"One of the blood witch scouts watching from the ferry

said that four women arrived by boat today," Zach said. "They didn't look like tourists. No gear or backpacks. They didn't speak to each other as they left the boat, either. Yolande suspects this is another party from Justine."

"Damn. I thought we'd have more time," she said.

"Nope. They're on their way, too. They rented a boat at one of the docks and headed south to take the long way around the island to reach us."

"How long have we got?"

"Not sure. We'll need more intel from Yolande's scouts. They're positioned along the coast to the south." Zach strapped himself into his Kevlar vest. "I'm going out with Yolande and another blood witch to wait for the boat to make landfall. Then we'll intercept them."

"What do you want me to do?" she asked, determined to help.

"It's good to have eyes everywhere. You could be a lookout and protect the coven," he suggested.

That seemed easy enough. She ran her fingertips along the rifle's scope. "Can I use the sniper rifle you got there?"

He picked up the Desert Tech Stealth Recon Scout. "You know how to use this?"

She took it from him, unloaded the .338 Lapua Magnum cartridge, and popped the clip back in. "Maybe. Just *maybe*."

He gave her a mischievous grin. "I thought your dad didn't want you to learn anything?"

"He didn't," she said wistfully. "I…learned a thing or two on my own through the Marksmen Club at the university. I haunted a gun range or two for four years. Not to say I'm a big deal or anything, but I'm a pretty good shot at three hundred yards."

Zach whistled with appreciation.

"Is that good?" Brian asked.

"I'm below average, to be honest," she admitted. "Most

of the weapons I've trained with are civilian issue." She eyed the gear on the table. "I don't know how to use half of this stuff, but I feel like I *should*." She tried to sound like she was joking but failed.

Zach drew her into his arms. "Giovanni wanted you to be happy."

"I know, but I can't fight my way out of a Dorito bag."

"You could shoot your way out?"

She rolled her eyes. "Not the same thing. When those hunters came to the hideout, I feared for my life. From now on, I want to be on the offensive versus the defensive."

The gear was stowed away, and Zach slung his pack over his shoulder. "You do realize most people don't have armed men storm their houses?"

"I still think every girl should be able to defend herself," Lark replied after giving him a sour look.

"I agree," Janet added.

They headed outside. The midafternoon sun peeked from behind thin clouds, but the snow wouldn't be melting anytime soon.

He turned to Lark with all seriousness. "I want you to keep Janet with you."

"Why? What's up?"

"The box."

She nodded. He didn't need to say anything else.

She shifted to head to the designated lookout point, but Zach snatched her hand to draw her back to him.

"No goodbye?" he murmured.

He kissed her lips long and hard.

No nibbles needed this time.

"I liked it," she admitted, "but I also like the anticipation."

His dark grin made her heart flutter. "I look forward to the challenge."

[20]

ZACH WAS RELIEVED HE WOULDN'T HAVE TO CONVINCE Lark to stay close to the coven's camp. He admired the fierceness in her eyes, but after his previous encounter with the blood witches, he feared what new tactics his adversaries would use.

Four paces ahead, Brian dipped his head to avoid low-hanging branches.

The full moon was weeks away—which meant they could run as pack—if they got over their issues. Whatever animosities existed, Zach would have to settle things between them. Whether that meant a full-on fight or just knocking Brian down a peg or two, he was prepared for what needed to be done.

"How are you holding up through all this?" See? Nobody could say he didn't make an effort through diplomacy instead of force.

Brian ignored him longer than necessary before he replied, "Good enough." He glanced at his cell phone again. Was in he in contact with Janet or something?

"You can't say this isn't more exciting than a nine-to-five job," Zach said. "I know I'd be bored."

"I'm sure you would've been bored if you were used to chasing after werewolves," Brian drawled.

Good Lord, this isn't the time.

So he knew about Zach's hunter past. No wonder Brian didn't trust him.

They'd reached the edge of the coven's property. The sky had darkened considerably—another storm was coming. That would hamper visibility. This wouldn't be the first time Zach would have to rely on his other senses.

At least they had the element of surprise on their side.

"Why do you tolerate that asshole?" Yolande mumbled.

"I can hear you, witch bitch," Brian yelled.

"Good," she spat. "Stop acting like an asshole then!"

"Why don't you tell her why I don't trust you, hunter?" Brian sneered.

"Hunter?" Yolande said with a smirk. "That does explain a few things."

Her nonchalant reaction angered Brian even further, and he stormed off to add distance between them.

"Sooner or later, you'll get what's coming to you," Brian mumbled.

Yolande's cell phone buzzed, and she picked up the call. Zach caught the conversation on the other end.

"The boat just passed me," the voice said. Most likely one of their younger witches, based on the high pitch and tremor. "They're still going north toward you."

"Understood. Stay safe, witchling, until the coven tells you to return home."

With the call completed, Yolande turned to Zach. "The boat is coming our way—"

"But we got a problem," he finished.

"You heard. Six witches instead of four."

A crack to the west made his head turn to the sound. He homed in on it while Yolande replied.

"I've faced double that number and survived, but I don't know their background or training."

He took a step away from Yolande. The forest around them was quiet again. Too quiet. In the distance, a click sounded.

The release of the safety on a weapon.

"Get down!" he roared, shoving Yolande to the ground. Bullets pinged off the trees where they had once stood.

Zach checked on Brian to find him behind a tree, his eyes squeezed shut.

Damn, he'd never been in a gunfight before.

"Do witches use guns?" Zach barked to Yolande as they scampered to the nearest cover.

"No, we usually don't. Maybe Justine hired an outside party!"

All this was a trap, then. Send a decoy to lure the soldiers away from the base.

Well played. Well played.

He retrieved a P30L from the holster strapped to his back, then crouched and darted toward the gunfire's origin.

Up ahead, he tracked multiple enemies, but the forest obscured their true positions. He stalked them from behind one tree to another.

As he drew closer to the first shooter, he expected to hear conversation, maybe even the voices of the witches as they exchanged information, but these attackers didn't speak.

Movement from his right alerted him to danger. He twisted with the gun—only to feel a nip hit his neck. Ice surged down his spine and his knees turned to dust. He gulped, but he couldn't feel the swallow as he collapsed.

His vision swam. With numb fingers, he plucked something from his neck: a hunter's tranquilizer dart.

Dread sliced through him.

The crunch of footsteps across the snow reached him. Someone was coming.

Get up, McGinnis.

Even the wolf within him howled and yipped, circling and wrestling the drugs dragging him toward unconsciousness.

A dark figure loomed above him, perched on one knee, and grasped his chin with her right hand. It was a woman. With her opposite hand, she waved at him, the red paw-print tattoo on her wrist flashing before his eyes.

"Nighty-night, McGinnis," the woman purred.

A HALF-HOUR PASSED.

Then a full hour.

Lark paced the alcove on the second floor of the Lake Haven house. She peered out the window into the gloomy night.

A strange feeling settled over her. Maybe it was anticipation. Her SRS lay ready right next to the window, and she'd executed two mock firing drills to prepare.

All she had to do was wait.

To keep herself sharp, she used the scope to scan the water for targets. Her heart wouldn't stop racing, but she wanted to be prepared for the moment where she'd have to fire and relive all the lessons during training.

Zach, where the hell are you? she thought. *Shouldn't we have heard something by now?*

For the third time, she looked over her shoulder to see Janet reading a book on the floor.

How she could read *Natural Birthing Techniques* at a time like this?

"Have you heard anything from them?" Lark asked her.

"Not a peep," Janet reported.

"We should've heard from them by now." She shook her head. "I don't like this. I should've asked Yolande for her cell phone number."

"Why haven't you reached out to Zach?" Janet asked.

Lark pursed her lips. "I've tried a couple times, but his phone is off. The man is superglued to it—even if he is in the middle of a fight, he'd find a way to contact us. Especially if the coven is in danger."

Janet slipped her glasses off. "Do you want me to reach out to one of the witches at the main house?"

The demon box and its effects immediately came to mind. There was no way Lark was letting Janet near that thing. "Don't worry about it. I got this. Let me go check in with Jamilah and see if she's heard anything."

Even though Lark didn't want Janet to set one foot near the main house, her guardian still waited on the Lake House back porch while Lark made her way there. No one stood guard in the back, but she spotted five blood witches waiting on the front porch, alert and ready to fight.

Jamilah approached her.

"Have you heard anything from them?" Lark asked her.

A flash of annoyance crossed the young woman's face, but she replied, "The last message I got was about fifteen minutes ago. She said something about how there were fewer people in the boat than when they first sighted them. After that, I haven't received any other messages."

Not the best news. "Can't we send someone out there to see what's going on?"

"I have strict orders to stay here. We are already outnumbered if a direct strike occurs, so it's in our best interest if we stand our ground here and wait for further instructions."

Lark bit back a curse. "Fine. You stay here. Where do I need to go?"

Jamilah sighed and rolled her eyes. From an inside pocket of her coat she pulled out a map and pointed out the last position Yolande had called from. "I can't give you anyone for backup, so you'll be on your own. Have you ever followed a map before?"

She didn't have to work hard to insult Lark, did she?

"I'll be fine. Text me if you hear from Yolande before I reach her." Lark gave Jamilah her cell phone number.

"Be careful, sister." The gruff comment still made Lark smile. At least the witch cared…a little.

She knew Zach's last location, but as to what she'd do when she got there, she'd figure things out on the fly. She raced back to Janet and told her of the change in plans.

"Are you sure about this?" Janet asked as she changed into a pair of boots and dark clothing.

Lark laughed drily. "I'm never sure about anything." They hurried southward, running at first, but then Lark found it difficult to run in the deeper snow.

Janet took point since she could see the farthest.

"If we run into danger, it's very important for you to stay behind me," Janet said, her voice low. "These witches can attack us from far away and up close. If what Brian, Zach, and I encountered a couple of days ago is what were about to face next, then none of this will be pretty."

Lark didn't have to be reminded after what she'd experienced when Phoebe attacked them. Now that she had the glyph book, she had an inkling of what a blood witch was capable of.

The thick clouds parted and the waning moon shone through cracks in the trees. Lark couldn't see much beyond a hundred yards in front of her.

Janet slowed down then paused to listen for danger.

"Do you see something?" Lark whispered.

"I smell nitroglycerin. Gunfire." Janet scanned the ground. "And something else."

Finally, Lark could see what Janet had noticed: footprints everywhere and broken branches. Had someone fought here?

She opened her mouth to call out Zach's name, but Janet snatched at her wrist and mouthed, "No."

Heart hammering in her chest, Lark followed Janet as the smaller woman left her side to trail a particular set of large footprints. Did they belong to Zach?

A couple of yards deeper into the woods, they came upon Yolande lying on her stomach. Lark hurried to roll her over.

"She's still breathing, and her heart is beating," Janet said calmly. "Check for any injuries while I search for the others. Don't leave this spot and stay quiet."

Lark nodded while she examined Yolande. Like any good patient, she grumbled the moment Lark checked her leg.

"You don't have to press so hard," she griped.

"Good to see you haven't lost consciousness," Lark said. "What the hell happened here?"

"I'm not sure. One minute we were standing there waiting for the witches to reach our position, and in the next, someone attacked us from the east. They had semiautomatic weapons, and we were forced to pull back and find cover." She winced when Lark checked her abdomen. So far Lark had only found a gunshot wound in her arm. Why hadn't Lark grabbed her backpack, as well as a basic medical kit?

Yolande cursed in French, and Lark held in a smile. "Are you trying to stab me or what?" Yolande grunted.

Lark pulled her belt off. "No, I'm trying to make sure you don't have any other injuries."

Right as Lark was checking Yolande's arm again, Janet reappeared with Brian. He had slung his arm over Janet's shoulder and limped along.

Zach, you better be halfway up a tree and sleeping up there, Lark thought. "Brian, where is Zach?"

"I asked him the same question, but he didn't answer," Janet said.

Brian's face went blank. Lark looked away, but she couldn't avoid the sucker punch to her gut.

"Where is he?" Lark repeated.

"We got squeezed," he reported. "Someone attacked us from the east. Zach…got pissed and chased after them."

Sounded like Zach. Always the hero.

Yolande tried to sit up, and Lark helped.

"Take it slow." She eased the enforcer halfway up.

"I'm a little dizzy, but I'll be fine," Yolande grumbled. "I've lost more blood than this before."

Lark sighed. "I had a feeling you'd say that."

Once Yolande was steady on her feet, Lark checked her phone. Still no messages from Zach. *What the hell, Z?*

While she called his number, Yolande reported to Jamilah. "We were ambushed, and the witches who attacked us retreated."

As Yolande limped to a tree to lean on it, Lark caught her yelling about how the "damn witches have guns now."

Had they always *only* used magic before against each other?

"According to Lark's guardian, the wolf is in pursuit," Yolande said. "Tell Zenobia the coven is secure—for now."

"What do you mean secure? We're not going after him?" Lark bolted after her.

The stubborn witch really had the nerve to turn her back on Lark.

Lark pelted her with arguments—how they should search a bit longer or check to see if Zach had reached the ferry.

No one was willing to help her.

She could've headed out alone, but she reluctantly

returned with them to the Painted Coven retreat. Returning to the houses took everyone far longer than she'd expected, as she and Janet each supported a wounded person. The houses' lights appeared right before midnight.

She half expected to see Zach waiting on the back porch with a smug smile on his face. *"I already caught the bad guys and you're just getting here?"* he'd say.

But no one was waiting.

She hurried into the house, checking near the door for his boots, searching around the kitchen table where he'd leave his pack, but there were no signs of him.

Janet and Brian joined her in the living room.

"He'll be fine," Brian reassured her as he limped to the couch and sat. "You know how he is. He has hunter training. He's probably following them back to Justine."

Lark shook her head. None of this made sense. Zach did stupid shit once in a while, but he rarely made tactical decisions that big unless he told others of his plans.

This was the guy who read *The Art of War* for shits and giggles.

A familiar feeling, fear, made her stomach ache. Her eyes watered. She blinked until her heart slowed.

He's not hurt. He'll return. He'll come back so I can cuss him out.

She stomped to the kitchen to prepare coffee. Time for a long watch. If Zach McGinnis really went after Justine—like an idiot—he'd have more trouble on his hands when he returned to her.

~

One Year & Three Months Ago

. . .

THE GRAVEYARD SHIFT AT THE HUNTING GROUNDS kicked in around midnight. On Tuesday nights past twelve, only the loneliest of souls remained at the pub.

A couple at the far end of the bar asked Lark to refill their glasses with Red Truck Lager before she locked up at one.

Her gaze kept flitting to the front windows. Each tall figure that passed made her think of *him*—from the college kids heading home to the couple walking hand in hand enjoying a cool summer night. Any of them could be Zach.

To keep herself from staring outside, she checked the bar. Nothing was out of place. Last week, she'd dusted off the spears and battle bows on the back wall. She even assessed the dartboards and pool tables—even though none of them needed to be replaced or repaired.

Now she considered hounding the other bartender on duty, but Ash eyed her antics with a rise of his right bushy white eyebrow.

"You might as well go home," the sixty-year-old former hunter said. "Those chairs you're trying to line up are still crooked."

Too late. He'd targeted her first.

"I'm just cleaning up," she said.

With a mischievous glint in his eyes, the Black man marched up to one of the seats she'd adjusted. He shoved the seat a couple of inches to the left.

How absolutely evil.

Now that he'd lovingly teased her, he ambled past her to take his usual spot behind the counter. The couple continued their small talk.

"Did you enjoy doing that?" she said with her hands on her hips.

"Maybe." He jerked his stubble-covered chin behind her. "Now you got something else to do."

She pivoted on her heel to see Zach standing there.

"Hey," he said.

The smooth hunter she'd met six months ago didn't wear the same easy smile. An evening hunting werewolves had left him with slouched shoulders and a darkening bruise on his cheekbone. He rarely wore caps—did the Vancouver Mounties baseball cap he wore cover more wounds? He limped to her. She recognized that walk. Whether the hunt had succeeded or failed, few escaped a mission without injury.

"Need a drink, Captain?" she asked softly.

When he finally stood before her, all the scenarios that had played out tonight in her head paused.

They wouldn't crash at her place and sleep—only to wake up to stumble to the hospital in the morning.

They wouldn't spend the day shuffling from Cynthia's room to her dad's.

In another world, another place, they'd share a couple drinks, a couple laughs.

In this other place, they'd venture to her apartment and eat ramen while watching comedy shows from the nineties.

The laughter continued until he reached for her and she reached for him. Their efforts to survive the next day wouldn't be hindered by the present.

But Lark and Zach didn't live in that fantasy world. As she wrapped her arms around him—gently—she was grateful that he'd returned to their *real* world.

It was far from perfect, but they were together, and that was all she'd ever need.

[21]

ANOTHER SPLASH OF ICY WATER HIT ZACH'S FACE. HE shivered as the water ran down his back and chest. He tried to tap into his senses, but the strange fog wouldn't lift.

Only the horrible cold remained—until minutes or maybe even hours later someone dumped frigid water over his head a second time.

"Wake up, McGinnis," the gravelly voice said. "Miranda might've mixed your cocktail a bit too harsh, but you should be up by now."

He blinked but couldn't focus on the opaque shapes moving in front of him. One standing. The other one sitting.

"I wanted to be sure we got him," a woman snapped.

"And we did—but he's useless to us if his heart or breathing stops," a middle-aged man replied.

The woman snorted. "I don't give a shit if he dies. He's vermin now."

The man's voice was clear—the clan sage Old Bart was here, but Zach hadn't heard the woman's voice in a while. An old acquaintance, perhaps?

He chipped away at the fog, gradually coming to his senses.

The events from last night swept through him. From the arrivals of the witches by ferry to the gunfire, and finally the blank spot.

His capture.

He swallowed a curse. Were any of the others here?

For some reason, his feet dangled off the ground. And they'd taken off his boots. A clever move on their part, since he had hidden weapons in them.

He tried to move, but his arms were tied and extended above his head. The strain on his stretched arms hurt like hell. He shifted his legs and found his feet had been bound with rope at the ankles.

So now what?

He glanced about to see he was inside one of the training trailers next to Lucas Lake. He'd been tied to the ceiling, and Old Bart sat on a stool not far from him.

"Long time no see," he whispered.

Bart sighed. He expected his mentor to frown, maybe glare and bark his disappointment until Zach's ears bled.

Instead, Bart stared, his blue eyes heavy with sadness.

"We shouldn't be sitting here like this, Zachary," he said.

"We shouldn't be, but like you always tell me, the winds don't always blow us to our intended shores." Zach tested the bonds on his wrists. The clan knew the exact tie to keep him bound.

"When I taught you to face adversity, I never meant succumbing to our enemies' temptation." Bart paused. "I expected better from you, which will make what we have to do to you so difficult."

The woman whose voice Zach hadn't recognized strolled before him. "Might be difficult for you, uncle, but I see this as a boon."

Old Bart's niece had his height, but where the clan sage had wise eyes, this dark-haired woman focused on him with harsh blue eyes. A scar along her chin and forehead indicated she'd survived a fight or two over the years, but she still had an eagerness in her stance only a fresh-faced hunter would have.

What the hell did she mean by that?

"A boon…and a moment I hadn't wanted to happen, Miranda," Old Bart added.

Zach took in the rest of the room. Behind Bart sat tables with the tools Zach was all too familiar with: pliers, hammers, silver-lined ropes, bags for choking. This particular trailer was used to prepare recruits for interrogation techniques.

The woman's name was familiar too. The last time he'd seen her, she'd made the decision to attend medical school and skip out on the hunter life for a while.

Guess she'd been unable to wait to be back in the business of *killing*.

Frustration pulsed in his chest, but he held himself in check. He'd waste precious energy wrestling with the ropes. The Red hunters weren't fools.

When his heartbeat settled, he found his voice. "I know what's about to happen. Let me go before this *ends* badly."

Miranda glanced at him with a smirk. "You were never much of a braggart, Zach. Don't start now." She strolled over to the nearest table and ran her fingertips over the tools. The standard intimidation tactic. "Should I fetch the students for this lesson?" she asked her uncle.

"Yes." Old Bart pinched his lips as he rubbed his face. "The sooner we learn what we need to know, the better."

"Don't do this," Zach whispered.

Miranda laughed. "Do what? Cut your *traitor* tongue out? That, I can do." She shook her head slowly. "All that talent wasted. Uncle Bart told me you were on track to lead the clan. What a joke." Her smile widened as she opened the trailer door to call in the recruits.

The young and fresh faces filed in. Ten in all, wearing military fatigues. Many of them were eager, their animosity evident in the way they edged closer to Zach.

Over ten years ago, he'd been one of them. Foolish and hungry to save the world. Though he was one of the smarter ones—he'd stood along the far wall and observed instead of leering. He relaxed, preparing himself for what was to come. If they wanted to push his buttons to make him talk, he'd make things interesting.

Old Bart began the interrogation. "You ready to talk, Wolf?"

"Are you ready to listen?" Zach asked. "'Cause I can't wait to tell you *everything*."

Miranda rolled her eyes, advanced on him, and punched him square in the jaw. His head snapped back hard enough for him to clench his teeth. Nice hit.

The mark on his jaw from her silver brass knuckles sizzled, but Zach didn't wince. "That tickles."

"The smart-ass routine will get you in trouble here," Miranda said darkly.

"Maybe." Zach's lip curled into a snarl. "But I remember you now. Should I tell them why you left for college instead of completing your hunter training?"

Miranda closed in on him, clutched a piece of his shirt, and pulled him forward. "If I weren't so merciful, you'd be full of bullet holes right now. Guess pain is the only thing you're interested in."

The blow to his side knocked the air out of Zach's lungs, but didn't do a damn thing to bring down his anger.

Miranda thrust her index finger in his direction. "You used to be hot shit around here, but not anymore. All the recruits used to look up to you. But look at you now. Your parents would be disgusted to see you like this."

She switched out the brass knuckles for pliers and stalked up to him with a glance at her uncle.

Old Bart said, "Where can we find the Windham pack's new hiding place?"

Ah, so that's what they wanted to know.

Zach slowly shook his head. After everything he'd been through—especially Cyn's illness—he shouldn't have expected better from them.

Guess all bets were off now.

AN EXPLOSION SHOOK THE HOUSE. LARK ROUSED HER from her sleeping spot on the living room couch.

What the hell was wrong now?

Another jolt reverberated through the house. She crashed hard onto the wooden coffee table and rolled to the floor. Ouch.

Janet rushed into the room from the kitchen. "Oh, shit." She glanced out the front room window. "We're under attack—"

Before she could finish, the windows imploded, sending glass and fragments into the room. Lark ducked.

Poor Janet took the brunt of it. She eased off the floor with cuts all over her face.

"Are you all right?" Lark crawled over to her.

"I've had better days," Janet said.

Brian rushed into the room from the kitchen. "What happened… Holy shit…"

They all turned toward the open windows to see a pontoon boat approaching between the reefs. Two determined witches stood in front, with others visible behind them.

"We got incoming," Lark yelled.

Brian took off his shirt. Janet slipped out of her jeans. They shuddered and spasmed as the change began. Lark stood there transfixed and stared at them as the roar of the oncoming boat grew louder.

Wake up, damn it. She took a deep breath and raced for the stairwell.

This fight is really about to happen.

At the top of the steps, she hurried to the window where the SRS was ready to go. She cracked open the alcove window and got into place.

The rifle rested against her shoulder. She briefly closed her eyes and prepared herself.

They want to capture you, she reminded herself. *Wound them first. Then shoot to kill if necessary.*

Through the scope, she spotted four witches getting dropped off at the main house, while the others docked at the pier in front of the Lake House.

Her guardians sped out of the front door and raced toward the stairwell leading to the pier.

She took aim at the nearest target: the woman using a talon on her fingertip to cut her hand. Then she drew an elaborate glyph on her palm. What spell was she casting?

Lark didn't wait to find out.

She blew out a breath and squeezed the trigger. The gun jolted in her hands. The reverberation rocked against her shoulder, but she was ready for it.

Pop. Pop. Pop.

The gunfire pushed the witches back until Lark caught movement to her right. The snake fluttered against her belly, then tightened until her breath caught. She stood.

Holy shit. Incoming.

Suddenly, the walls and windows blew inward. She waited for the explosion to send her sprawling, but a shimmering concave light flickered in front of her. The light disappeared as the tattoo quieted.

A shield of some type.

But would it happen again?

Through the open window, she looked over to the Mountain Haven House to see where the attack had originated. One of the witches on the wharf glared at Lark. Another witch in the party stood in front, redirecting the rocks rising from the waters. Where had the rocks come from?

It was Yolande. The redhead's face showed strain as her focus jumped from one place to another. One boulder covered in algae rose. Then another, and another. The rocks from the opposing parties collided in midair. They fell to the water with a hard splash.

Yolande's face paled, but she kept the barrage going.

Lark didn't miss the trail of blood dripping down Yolande's neck.

Meanwhile, her guardians in wolf form plowed into the two witches in front of the Lake House. The women's screams were swallowed by growls and yips.

She had to act somehow. This fight was far from done, and Yolande couldn't hold the line forever. From her left, Lark spied a rock sailing in her direction.

Oh shit. No time like the present.

She leapt out of the way before the rock smashed into the house and hit the wall on the other side of the alcove. Once the path was clear, she hurried down the steps with the rifle in hand. Damn, she wished she'd asked for something smaller. A Glock 26 would do. If necessary, her bare hands would work.

She sidestepped debris once she got to the ground floor. The battle continued to rage outside. Fear danced up her spine. Was this what her father had felt every time he dared to chase after werewolves? This tingling in his chest, while his stomach churned so much that he thought he'd lose his lunch?

She almost raced outside but remembered her marksman training. Find the ideal locations to take aim. Time wasn't on her side, but she spied ideal spots on the porch with minimal cover behind urns.

As if those urns would stop projectiles like those rocks.

With little choice, she crouched and made her way out the broken front door to the porch. Behind the cover of the shrubbery, she peeked out.

Yolande was on her knees and breathing heavily. The four witches on the boat had advanced up a flight of steps.

Why hadn't Yolande taken out the steps?

And damn, Lark didn't have a clear line of sight to take anyone out. She'd have to leave her cover for a better strike point.

Fuck.

Two witches were now on the offensive, while the other two took a defensive position. She searched for her guardians. The dark wolves had disappeared—then she spotted them on the other side of Mountain Haven House. They prowled toward the witches, their heads low as they darted from one hiding spot to the other.

But they wouldn't make it in time.

A strange hum filled the air as two massive boulders began to rise from the water a hundred feet out. Were they a last-ditch effort from Yolande? No, her attention darted from left to right as she anticipated the incoming attacks.

Do something, damn it, Lark thought. She willed the tattoo to intervene, but the serpent lay still. Fine. Lark stepped off the porch. She'd give those bitches another target if necessary.

No more games, you little, slimy shit, she thought. *Help me.*

She clenched her fists tight. Then tighter, until her forearms strained.

What had Fredda said? That the demon fed off suffering. That Lark could harness it, but she'd have to feed it herself.

Lark had to survive if she wanted to find Zach.

She pressed the thumb of her right hand into the soft spot between her left hand's thumb and index finger. The spot was still bandaged—and sore—so it hurt like a motherfucker, drawing a hiss from her lips. But the serpent sprang to life. There. She could feel it stirring, writhing against her back and belly.

The boulders rose until the bottoms could be seen.

The snake tattoo coiled, preparing to strike. She pressed harder. The pain forced a cry from between her lips, but she focused on the sea. Beyond the two rising boulders to the deeper waters.

Instead of letting the snake strike forward, she made it *pull.* Tug *inward.*

She closed her eyes. Felt the sheer weight of the water. Felt the ever-increasing pain. The snake squeezed her midsection until she released her grip on her hand. When she opened her eyes, she had a split second to blink before the oncoming wave washed her off her feet.

WHEN ZACH DIDN'T ANSWER QUICKLY ENOUGH, Miranda pinched his pinky hard with the pliers. Pain rocketed up his hand, forcing him to suck in breaths through clenched teeth.

But he didn't say a word.

Miranda clutched his chin, but she couldn't jerk his face toward her. He wouldn't give her that satisfaction.

"Should I do your tongue next?" she snapped.

Heat pulsed through him. He fixed his eyes on her and did nothing to contain the raw growl that gathered in his chest.

Miranda trembled as she scrambled back.

The once-eager students' faces fell.

"Why don't you come for my tongue?" he said, his voice low and ragged. "Seems like you're willing to act without considering the consequences."

His incisors lengthened. Claws bit through his fingertips. The wolf circling inside of him hungered to show them what they should truly fear. *Him.*

"Is he trying to get away?" one student murmured.

"He can't. Those are reinforced ropes on his wrists," Miranda snapped. She closed in on Zach with the hammer. "Tell us what we want to know…or maybe we should ask Lark?"

Rage pulsed through him, but he checked himself.

Damn it, they had to know about her if they'd captured him.

When he continued to struggle against the bonds, Miranda punched him again. When that got no reaction out of him, she reached back with the hammer and smashed it into his hand.

The pain was immediate and utterly horrific, but the crunch of his bones was satisfying. He let the pain course through him—his growl of pain fed the need to begin the final transformation.

Face red and lips pinched together, Miranda struck him again, until Old Bart snatched her wrist.

"Are you in control?" he shouted. "Miranda?"

But it was too late.

Before the muscles in his hand could re-form themselves, Zach slipped it out of the bond. The moment his hand was released, he waited a split second for the bones to re-form and then freed his other hand.

With a thud, he hit the floor in a crouched position. He freed his feet next.

"Lesson time, hunters," he whispered.

He snarled and rammed Miranda, sending her crashing into the nearest table. As she tried to shove a Taser into his side, he grasped her arm and flipped her hard onto her back.

"Seize him!" Old Bart snapped. Using a comm on his shoulder, he yelled, "McGinnis is loose. Send backup!"

Several students surged toward Zach, grabbing weapons from the table. The reluctant ones scrambled for the door.

Those were the wise ones.

They tried to surround him, but he picked up Miranda and hurled her in their direction. Two hunter boys jumped out of the way, and she crashed in a heap to the floor.

Minus five points for team building.

He yanked the hammer out of the nearest hunter's hand with a twist of his wrist. With a shove, he pushed a girl back. The next attacker, a fresh-faced hunter with pockmarks all over his face, got the same treatment for swinging his knife. Zach threw that toy into the nearest wall. Four more hunters tried to attack. He could see the move before the swing occurred. Each slight twist in their torso before they struck telegraphed their plans to him.

Cyn had remarked how former hunters would make deadly werewolves, but he had no idea what she'd meant.

Until now.

Every adversary tried to anticipate his moves, but he was always a step ahead. Their training showed.

They expected him to run. To cower against the wall and protect himself.

What they hadn't expected was for him to stand his ground and fight.

More hunters—the experienced ones wearing tactical gear—surged through the door, weapons ready.

He caught the clicks of safeties releasing. Then the noises around him disappeared. Only the wolf remained, focusing with cold accuracy on the prey around him. Eight targets. Tiny, fragile hearts pounding. Their breaths quick and panicked. The stench of their fear blanketed the air. He savored it.

In three swipes, he could cross the room and slit all their throats. The muscles in his legs tensed up. Instead of shifting toward his first target, he snarled and plowed through the hunters blocking the door. They were tossed aside like scattered marbles. A second later, he stood before the door and leapt outside.

I am not the monster they believe me to be.

What I believed I would be.

He ran hard. Briefly, he searched for the sun, seeing it high in the sky to his right. North lay ahead.

Gunfire erupted behind him and hit the ground near his feet. He darted behind the nearest tree before he sprinted off again. A part of him knew he should find the nearest pier with a boat. He should steal the boat and get the hell off the island. That would be the only way to protect Lark from the hunters.

But then again, they knew where she was. They would use her against him, even if her father was a hunter. None of that mattered. Only his betrayal and their loss.

He'd have to face the Red clan this time.

All his life, he'd been taught to protect his brothers and sisters in arms. Teach them. Cultivate them.

But if they wanted a war, they'd fucked with the wrong man.

[22]

LARK WOKE UP TO THE SETTING SUN BATHING HER FACE through a window. She could barely move. It was as if she'd run for miles, only to keep pushing for many more and collapsed afterward.

Had the demon done this to her?

Slowly, she turned her head to see Janet sitting in a chair beside her bed. Her head was slumped to the side as she slumbered. Not far behind her, Brian snored against the back wall.

Lark held in a sigh as sleep tried to tug at her senses.

Rest, her body implored.

Even the serpent lay still, but she couldn't sleep now. So much had happened. Had everyone survived the attack?

The crash and rumble of the boulders falling from the skies flashed through her mind. She'd feared for her life. She'd depended on Zach to stand beside her and protect her.

I stood alone before; I can do it again, she thought.

As hard as she tried not to think about him, his face was still there in the back of her mind. His smirk. The way he ran his fingers through his hair to keep the longer strands out of his face. She tried to hold on to what made him Zach, but she couldn't help but think about the witches' powers. If Zach had truly gone after them, would he have survived?

Or did his promise to always return to her mean nothing?

Lark tried to rest for a bit longer, but a knock on her door made Janet rise to answer it.

"Who is it?" Lark whispered.

Before Janet opened the door, she said, "It's Yolande."

Lark sighed with relief to know the enforcer had survived.

Yolande entered the room, not as quickly as her usual brisk business pace. Even her lips appeared paler than usual.

"Hey," Lark said.

Yolande gave a slight nod. "The elders wanted me to check on your condition."

Lark eased herself into sitting up. "Not too bad. Why do I feel so drained?"

"Every spell has a price. I pay in blood. You pay another toll," Yolande explained. "Your vitality."

Lark nodded. "Did I really move all that water inland?"

Yolande chuckled. "Yes, you did, and you saved us all."

"The witchlings are safe?"

That question made Yolande's harsh features soften. "Yes, my daughter and the other girls are safe, but the property is a bit banged up."

"I can only imagine." Lark turned to sit on the side of the bed.

"There is something I need to tell you," Yolande said, "but first you should know that one of Justine's soldiers survived."

That made Lark lean forward. "Where are the elders keeping her?"

"Bound and locked up in a room. Don't worry, we have her under control."

"What are you going to do with her?"

"We will question her later—there's another matter you should know." Yolande lowered her voice. "And you're not going to like it."

"What's going on?" Lark asked as Janet joined her on the bed.

"It's about the attack in the woods," Yolande said. "For the life of me, I couldn't believe a witch would use a firearm."

"Is it against the rules or something?" Janet asked.

"No, but every single coven I've lived within never used them. They're not as effective against possessed witches."

"So that means the people who attacked you guys weren't blood witches," Lark said evenly.

"They were hunters. And I think Brian knew it," Yolande said. "He said, 'Sooner or later, you'll get what's coming to you.' Then he conveniently disappeared while we were attacked."

Janet bit her lower lip and used a rubber band to draw her hair out of her face. "He said that because he hates that Zach used to be a hunter."

"That's crazy," Lark said. "Why would a werewolf go to hunters to strike a deal?"

Janet pursed her lips. "Because it's all a power play." She snorted, her disgust clear on her face. "Brian has resisted Zach's authority from the get-go…and the only way to get rid of the alpha in any pack is to kill him or have someone *else* do it."

Lark's chest tightened. "And the Red hunters are right in our backyard. Where is Brian?"

"He's on guard duty outside the house."

Lark rose, but Janet stopped her. "You're not planning to

confront him, are you?" Janet barely reached Lark's shoulder, but held her firmly.

"Fuck yes, I am."

"We need to play this carefully," Yolande said. "For all we know, he may know where Zach is being held. If we corner him, he may withhold information."

Lark shook her head with disbelief. "I can't believe this. We're not exactly a pack or a family, but we look out for each other."

"So, we wait?" Janet asked Yolande.

What good would waiting do? Zach could be trapped somewhere on the island—or even worse, dead. Lark's stomach soured at the thought, and the tat responded by finally moving.

No, she had to believe she had a chance to find him and help somehow. If Brian fucked up, then he'd make amends or get the hell away from her.

But how would she pry the information out of him?

An idea came to mind, and she glanced down at Janet's hand. "I'm in control now. You can let go of me."

Janet gave a dry laugh and released her. "You still smell pissed enough to launch him into space."

As Lark slipped on a pair of sneakers, she said, "I hope he's prepped his flight suit."

A couple of minutes later, Lark, followed by Janet and Yolande, left the Lake House to step onto the back porch.

Anger drove her toward him until she took in the debris everywhere. The shorter maple, pine, and cedar trees were bent over, while the low-lying plants were uprooted and scattered everywhere. Even the deck furniture and potted plants were missing.

She'd caused all this? How much water had she pushed inland?

Lark made a beeline to Brian standing at the edge of the courtyard.

"You're awake," he said with a smile. But that smile faded when she got closer.

Did he smell her fury? *Good.*

"What's wrong?" He looked from her to the other two women waiting by the house.

"Did you think I'd never find out what you did?"

His jaw slackened. "What do you mean?"

"You gave Zach to the Red hunters, didn't you?"

Brian licked his lips. "Is that what Yolande told you? Do you believe her?"

Lark folded her arms to keep herself from wrapping her hands around Brian's neck. "You didn't answer my question," she said slowly.

Brian glanced over her shoulder. "No," he vehemently whispered.

"Should I have you answer that question in front of Janet?"

Brian let out a long, slow breath.

A werewolf would smell his lie with ease.

"I did it for your own good," he finally admitted.

Lark took a step back and bit her lower lip. She'd heard that phrase before. And she was pretty damn tired of folks "helping" her. Her dad had done it, Zach had stayed away from her because of it, and now Brian had jumped into the conga line.

She advanced on him and poked her index finger into his chest. "No, you did it for you."

He sighed. "He would've endangered all of us—"

"Where is Zach?" she snapped. The serpent demon flared to life and twitched on her back.

"He's gone."

Lark stared him down, but his stony expression infuriated her further. Even worse, Brian turned his back on her.

Insolent wolf, the demon said to her. *Kill it and smear its insides along the mountainside.*

She clenched her fists to fight the temptation. Gutting Brian wouldn't fix this.

But it sure would scare the shit out of him.

The serpent coiled around her torso as if offering encouragement.

He'll betray you again, the serpent advised her. *End him now.*

"Guess that means I have only one choice, then," she whispered. "Brian, we're done."

His face went ashen. "What?"

"You are no longer my guardian."

ZACH VENTURED AS CLOSE AS HE COULD DARE TO LARK, right at the edge of the witches' wards. Yolande had hinted at their location, and he remembered well.

With a single step, he could cross between the cluster of pine trees before him, but the witches would know he'd returned.

He couldn't go back yet. Returning here would bring the Red hunting clan to Lark's doorstep, and he didn't want to defend two fronts. Not yet.

Zach waited as long as he could. After running all morning, he'd followed the standard procedure to elude prey. He'd covered his tracks as best as he could by doubling back multiple times, setting new paths through the Fairy Fen Nature Reserve, and circling to throw the hunters off his trail.

He shivered in the cold, recalling how he'd bathed in a

creek to the south of here. The hunters would use dogs whenever possible.

But what he wondered was whether they would assume he'd stay on the island or leave.

Zach sighed and took two steps away from the wards. His time was almost up.

Only so many choices sat before him, but those options for action depended on how the hunters played things out.

He considered the dark look on Miranda's face and Old Bart's steadfastness, then turned away from the coven's land and ran hard to the east.

To keep Lark safe, he'd have to play the hunters' game. If he knew Old Bart, reinforcements were coming. Zach would need to line up a few chess pieces for this game to advance to checkmate.

CRIPPEN REGIONAL PARK WRAPPED AROUND THE PIER to Horseshoe Bay and provided minimal cover. At around midday, traffic along Grafton Road through the middle of the park was minimal.

All Zach had to do was head east and he'd find the ferry back to the mainland, but he had other issues to tackle before he ventured that way: he needed clothes.

Without any money or even a phone to access his online accounts, he'd have to get creative.

Instead of traveling out in the open along Grafton Road, he stuck to the cover of the trees in the northern part of the park. In the distance, he could hear the sounds of cars, smell home-cooked food and exhaust fumes.

He trekked southeast through the trees until he spotted his target: the Bowen Island Visitor Information Centre.

One thing he did know during his travels was that adults

and kids dropped shit all the time—whether it was coats, hats, or toys.

He waited for a small party to leave through the front before he darted inside. A friendly receptionist behind a desk looked up with surprise.

"Can I help you?" she said tentatively.

He had to imagine he didn't look or smell too good. His T-shirt had a few tears, but at least his jeans were in one piece.

"Hi, my wife left her coat in here yesterday," he said. "Do you mind if I check the lost and found, please? It's got my son's favorite toy inside, and he'd be upset if I didn't find it."

The blonde scrunched her nose up. Yeah, bathing in the creek might not have been the best idea.

"Sure, the bin is near the restroom." She looked back at the book she was reading.

Zach strolled through the visitor center's main room until he spotted the hallway to the restrooms. The bin she'd referred to sat between the doors to the respective bathrooms.

Bingo.

Ten minutes later, Zach walked out of the visitor center wearing a black University of Montreal hoodie and some sad-looking gym shoes. Whoever had left them behind had huge feet, but at least Zach wouldn't be spotted walking around barefoot.

With his hands stuffed in his pockets and the hood over his head, he made his way toward the Snug Cove Terminal. Around this time of the day, there should be another ferry arriving or leaving. Either of them should give him the traffic he needed.

All around him, vacationers dressed in winter coats milled around, excited about returning home after a morning spent on the island. It was easy to spot the residents versus the sightseers.

He waited patiently near the gate to the ferry with his chin tilted down, but his eyes and nose alert for danger. It didn't take long for hunters to appear. Two pulled up in the pier parking lot in a truck. The dudes weren't hard to identify. They searched the lot for him the minute they got out.

Hadn't they learned not to be so obvious?

Cars leaving the island lined up as a ferry pulled up for the next set of passengers. The hunters circled through the lot, and Zach waited.

Once the hunters were close enough, he walked toward the line and flowed into the outgoing passenger queue.

As expected, he caught the grunt from one of the hunters. "There he is," one said to the other.

The line continued past the cars as folks headed toward the ferry. Another line of cars on the opposite side of the road had departed the ferry and now made its way onto the island. Through a car rearview mirror, Zach could see the hunters peeking around the ten people behind him.

The ticket taker loomed ahead.

Zach passed two trucks then, when he came to a boat hitched to an RV, slipped to the side and darted behind the RV.

"Where did he go?" he heard one hunter whisper as he circled the boat on the opposite side.

"Check around the boat," the other replied. "He probably climbed inside."

Once his trackers were occupied checking the boat and RV, Zach made it to the woods off Grafton Road.

From his position on a hill overlooking the pier and the bay, he observed the hunters completing their search. He couldn't resist grinning when they made a rushed phone call, then hurried onto the ferry.

Now that the hunters believed he'd left, he had one more task to complete.

[23]

Night brought clear skies and below-freezing temperatures. Instead of staring out the window to see the snow falling over the ocean, Lark had the most *delightful* view of plywood slabs.

At least the plywood kept her from seeing the traitor.

"Has Brian left yet?" she'd asked Janet while they boarded the upstairs windows.

"No, he's rooted to the same spot."

Lark suspected Janet pitied him. She didn't blame Janet for her loyalty, but right now she refused to forgive him, especially if Zach was in danger.

She didn't have to sit in the Mountain Haven House great room for very long. Yolande beckoned her to join the elders in a small room next to the front door.

Lark peered around the space and found an empty room with slate-gray walls, a cot with dark red blankets, and a chair. Their prisoner crouched in the corner with her hands and ankles bound. Fredda, Zenobia, and Iluminada waited for Lark inside.

The dark-haired witch with a bob haircut glanced up at

Lark and smiled. Lark didn't return the gesture and joined the others.

"Interrogation time?" the witch asked in a high-pitched voice. "What methods will you use this time, Fredda? Will you make me see my dead son again?"

Lark glanced at Fredda to see her pinching her lips together.

"You shouldn't have come here, Katia," Zenobia said softly. "The rest of your friends are dead."

When Katia didn't speak, Zenobia added, "Where is Justine?"

Katia gave a half-smile, revealing large front teeth. "Does it matter? Whether you go to her or she comes to you, Justine *will* have her way."

Zenobia laughed. "You're nothing but an opportunistic traitor."

"Answer the question," Yolande snapped.

"The world has changed," Katia said to Zenobia. "Deep pockets feed hungry mouths like mine. Not all covens are as *comfortable* as yours." Her black eyes darted to Lark. The weight of her gaze pushed Lark toward the wall.

The prisoner added, "And look at you. The bodies are already stacking up around here. You're just as powerful as Justine claimed you'd become."

"Powerful?" Lark scoffed. "You're kidding me, right? You attacked me first. No one would've died—"

"Our cause is righteous," Katia countered. "Today, you'll knowingly kill a handful, but in months, you won't be able to control yourself. Folake thought she could resist, but over time, she weakened. You're caught up in a circle now. Your killing will never end."

Folake's words when she'd given Lark the tattoo came to mind: *"You follow the circle now."*

"Shut up!" Fredda said.

Katia ignored her and continued to spew her venom in Lark's direction. "The cycle will end when Justine kills you. Just like she *killed* Folake."

Katia's words swept through the room and sucked the breath from Lark's lungs: Folake was dead. Her only chance to return the tattoo was gone.

Wide-eyed, Zenobia kneeled before Katia and grabbed her chin. "You lie! Why would Justine attack Folake if she doesn't have the demon anymore?"

Katia's smug smile faded. "Because our fight with the blood demons will end when the serpent no longer has a haven. We have to believe that. Every one of her kindred spirits *must* die for us to live."

"Zealot garbage," Yolande spat. "There's no literature connecting the blood demons to the inked ones. Our ancestors were foolish enough to let them in. Getting rid of a few won't flush all the trash down the drain."

Katia slowly shook her head. "How do you know? What if she's the key to our freedom? A world without the blood demons would set us free."

Lark held her breath while she glanced around the room. Did any of them believe Katia? All the witches glared at the prisoner.

The bound witch focused on Lark. "If you killed yourself, you could end everything. The witches would be free. The wolves, too. What happened to your mother would never happen again—"

Lark advanced on her. "Don't you dare mention my mother."

"You didn't tell her, Zenobia?" Katia said. "That's a pity."

Lark stole a glance at the elder witch, who said nothing.

Katia continued, her voice speeding up. "You didn't know that Lupita was Folake's kindred spirit, did you? Your mother ran away from the coven and tried to hide in the outside world. She ended up falling in love with a man and getting pregnant." She smacked her lips to emphasize the final word. "Folake wanted to do the exchange, but an unborn child has never survived the process. To protect you, Lupita continued to hide with her hunter, but in the end, the werewolves cleaned up the mess for us."

"Shut your filthy mouth!" Zenobia snapped.

Suddenly, the lights in the room flickered. Iluminada, Fredda, and Yolande backed away from Zenobia as her light blue eyes turned black. Katia screamed as her eyes did the same.

The prisoner shuddered and fell on her side.

Lark staggered backward. The world around her spun as her hands went numb.

"Oh, *mi hija*." Iluminada wrapped her arms around Lark. "I'm so sorry."

"Did you know?" she whispered.

"We suspected Folake was her kindred spirit, but we never had any proof…"

Lark collapsed against the wall. Katia continued to beg for her eyesight.

But all Lark could focus on was the churning and twisting of the demon serpent as it fed on her suffering.

THE MIDNIGHT WIND BLEW SNOWDRIFTS UP TO THE trees. Zach used the snowfall to obscure him while he crept along the hunter camp outskirts. This late at night, only two guards monitored the camp's four trailers.

They didn't have a reason to assign more sentries.

In the darkness, he smiled. Hadn't their target left the island for the mainland?

So far, he'd slipped past their tripwires and chuckled at

their perimeter alarms. Of course, this camp trained students, but he'd expected the teachers to run a tighter ship.

Even though he'd gotten in easily, he still had to be careful. Searchlights illuminated areas around the four trailers comprising the camp, but too many places between the buildings were dark.

He snuck around the outer perimeter until he found what he was looking for: the supply depot. Since this installation served as a training site, he doubted he'd find much, but after breaking through the sad-ass locks, he uncovered the basics to keep him going: boots, winter wear, and standard-issue tactical gear.

The hunters had taken his body armor, but at least he wouldn't be running around and fighting in flannel.

Steps approached him from the opposite side of the depot. The sentry was coming. Zach hurried to finish gathering supplies and left the depot toward the northeast.

Suddenly, the searchlights in the base shifted to the west. What did they find?

From the safety of the trees, he peered out to see Brian darting back into the cover of the forest.

Zach cursed. What was Brian doing here?

Then a thought came to mind: if Brian was here, was Lark nearby?

He raced toward Brian, taking a long path around Josephine Lake to intercept him. It didn't take long to cross the wolf's path.

The moment Zach closed in on Brian, he tackled him to the ground.

There was no animosity on Brian's face. Lark's guardian looked at Zach once, then turned away with shame.

Zach stood over Brian for the longest time before he spoke. He didn't want to hear the answer if Lark was hurt—or worst of all, dead.

"What are you doing here?" Zach folded his arms. He hoped for a good answer before he unloaded bullets into Brian.

"For hours I've been searching for you," Brian admitted.

"And now you've found me." Zach tugged on Brian's arm until he stood. "Why are you here and not with Lark?"

Brian scanned the ground as if searching for the words to say. "She exiled me."

Zach wanted to quip, "I wonder why," but instead he waited. If Lark had released Brian from guarding her, that meant she suspected he was behind the Red clan ambush.

Relief filled Zach's chest.

She was alive and still clever as ever.

"You sold me out, man," Zach said evenly. "What do you think I can do for you?"

Brian swallowed, and his Adam's apple bobbed a few times. "You could talk to her. If she sees you're alive, she'll—"

"Forgive you? I don't want to forgive you either."

Brian sank to his knees, rested his hands in his lap, then bared his neck in submission.

Zach turned his back on him. Brian's surrender was to Lark, not him.

"Please, I don't know what to do," Brian said. "Every time I think about running away, I feel this incredible sense of loss." He shuddered. "I know it's the magic that ties me to her, but I thought… I felt like she needed me, and I knew what was best for her."

Zach adjusted the pack on his shoulder and set off again. Anger should've flared within him, but that raging fire had long been extinguished. Right after what he'd experienced this morning, he would've torn Brian's throat out and let his carcass feed the wildlife. But Zach's rage was funneled elsewhere.

He caught the sounds of Brian standing and shuffling after him. "Where are you going?"

"To do what needs to be done without *compromising* the mission or my friends."

Brian stood and trailed him. "I'm coming too."

[24]

Lark wanted to bury her head under her bed covers, maybe even listen to some music to think of anything but the outside world, but she decided to get her hands dirty instead.

For real.

Justine's attacks had slowed down the coven's day-to-day activities, but maintaining the greenhouse remained. According to Fredda, one of the sources of their organic produce came from the heated structure.

For the next two hours, Lark helped Jamilah and a few of the older witchlings pluck out the weeds from the herbs. The activity was mundane—and even the younger witches made fun of how often she uprooted the mint versus removing the crabgrass.

"Have you ever gardened before?" a fair-haired girl asked.

"Not really," Lark admitted. "The closest my dad got to pulling vegetables was taking the tomatoes and pickles off his burgers from McDonald's."

That got a laugh out of them. By midday, Jamilah declared Lark's work was done and shooed her off. She reluctantly left the greenhouse to see two men standing at the edge of the clearing.

Was she seeing things? She took one tentative step forward before she broke out into a run.

He'd returned.

She jumped into his arms and wrapped her legs around his waist. He held her up so she could get a good look at him, but he dodged her inspection to lean forward. The moment their lips met, all the cold around her disappeared.

She even caught the girls giggling in the greenhouse.

"Is that her boyfriend?" one girl asked.

"Probably," Jamilah said with annoyance. "He better be."

Once Zach set her down, Lark whispered, "Where have you been all this time?"

Zach jerked his head toward Brian. Her former guardian wouldn't meet her eyes.

"We'll talk about it later." Zach took her hand. "Let's get inside. I'm starving."

They'd made it halfway across the courtyard before Zach turned around.

"Move it, Brian," Zach said.

The werewolf stood rooted to the spot with his hands stuffed in his pockets.

"Have you forgotten what he did to us?" Lark asked.

"That's between Brian and me," Zach said.

To her surprise, Zach and Brian exchanged a long look before her former guardian plodded up after them.

Once they entered the Lake House kitchen, Brian didn't say a thing and sat next to the kitchenette.

From her spot reading a paperback at the counter, Janet gave Brian a side-eye.

"What's going on?" she mouthed to Lark.

Lark shrugged. Last night, she'd told herself that if Brian

dared to speak to her, she'd launch nukes from orbit to take him out.

While the guys chatted quietly, Lark prepared seafood wraps for lunch. She sensed the weight of Zach's gaze on her back. Briefly, she turned to peek to see him giving her that *look*: his body was relaxed against the seat, but his half-closed eyes watched every move she made.

As if she were prey he couldn't wait to capture.

Heat warmed her cheeks. The pleasant feeling fluttered down to her stomach.

It was good to have him back.

"Come help set the table," Janet called.

Brian cleared gear and books off the table while Zach approached Lark. She'd finished the final wrap. He stretched out behind her to reach for the plates.

"Excuse me." His chest bathed her back in heat. She swallowed hard against the desire to arch her back against him. If she tilted her head to the left just right, he could kiss her, but he grabbed what he needed and returned to the table.

Horny much? she thought with amusement.

She'd just gotten him back and she was ready to ride him into the sunset. Lark had so many questions—what had happened to him, in particular.

The four of them sat down to eat.

Zach sat to her left, pulling his chair close to hers until their shoulders and thighs touched. A smile crossed her lips. Zachary McGinnis wasn't helping her libido.

They ate in silence until Zach relayed what had happened to him. She'd thought she was prepared to hear it all. Especially how the Red clan had captured Zach and interrogated him to make him reveal the Windham pack's position. Her frustration with Brian only intensified—until Zach slipped his right hand into hers. He squeezed gently. The softening of his eyes and brief upward tilt of lips calmed her.

I'm here now.

He probably didn't want her to be mad, but Brian had set a series of events in motion that might make them leave Bowen Island.

Once Zach finished, Janet asked, "Will the Red clan come looking for you?"

"I made sure I covered my tracks," Zach replied. He recounted his time at the Snug Cove ferry.

Lark took a deep breath. "But how long will they search the mainland before they return to look for you here?"

"I don't know," he admitted. "But what I do know is my former clan is tenacious. Old Bart rarely advises his hunters to back down from a fight."

The weight of his words left Lark's lunch heavy in her stomach. How long did they have before Justine attacked them from one direction and the hunters from another?

A caress along her knee to her inner thigh reminded her of the man sitting next to her. Zach leaned his head toward hers. His breath tickled her ear.

"Come with me," he whispered.

Anticipation drew her away from the kitchen. Urgency pushed her up the stairwell. Soon they would be alone again, and she couldn't think of much else.

Once her bedroom door shut, she ran her hands down the stubble along his chin while he stared at her. His hold was firm, as if he'd never let her go.

She'd never felt so adored.

"Are you hurt?" she whispered.

He shook his head. "Not anymore." Slowly, she reached to take off her T-shirt, but he said, "Dance with me."

She gave him a small smile. "Why?"

He reached for her phone on the end table. What was he

doing? She opened her mouth to protest, but the moment she heard Sam Smith singing the opening of "Lay Me Down," her heart melted. She grinned and settled her head against his chest.

Yes, she'd longed for this. She'd longed to just *be* with him.

"This song always reminds me of us," he whispered against the top of her head.

"Me too."

She swayed to the music, feeling the words of melancholy and sorrow. They'd been apart for too long.

"I want you so badly," he said, drawing a shiver from her. "But I slowed things down 'cause I'm afraid I'll be too rough."

"It's okay," she whispered. "I'm not fragile anymore."

She could barely finish before his mouth crashed down on hers. They reached for each other to undo buttons, yank down zippers. Everything came off until they stood naked. No more barriers existed between them. The only thing that mattered was to find bare skin to kiss, to stroke, to nip.

She ran her hands up his wide back, memorizing every dip and curve. To her joy, she got a hiss from him as her fingers played over the firm muscles of his ass. He was perfection.

Her head grew heavy when their tongues connected. She wanted to be open to everything he had to offer.

Feeling him clutch her backside and reach for her buttocks to draw her against him made her moan.

Suddenly, he picked her up and carried her to the bed. He laid her down in the middle.

On her stomach, of all places.

Where did he plan to touch her first?

His tongue stroked the sensitive skin of her upper back. She arched her back as each exquisite kiss and lick sent her into a frenzy. He drifted from one stop to another. Her lower back. Her right buttocks.

And finally, he spread open her legs, drew her hips upward, and licked her *there*.

"Zach…" She repeated his name again and again as his tongue darted inside of her.

Soon he had her panting. Begging. Then he withdrew.

He stretched on top of her, supporting his weight with one arm while his erection pulsed against her opening.

He was right where she wanted him. She hungered to be claimed. Marked.

She parted her thighs, but he slid out of the way. *So it's like that, huh?*

She squirmed, every nerve ending within her firing as he sucked at her neck. All the while, his length pulsed and dipped.

He was controlling the tempo and pace, but she didn't want him to be gentle.

She needed him to always be there.

Touching her.

Reminding her he wouldn't leave again.

When he entered her hard and fast, her exhale was one of relief and bliss. They were one again. She clenched the pillows and accepted everything he had to offer.

Then he turned her over. They were face to face again. Chest to chest. One heartbeat.

HE COULD STARE AT HER ALL DAY, BUT RIGHT NOW SHE was the most beautiful with her lips parted, her cheeks flushed with passion, and her hair messy and spread over the pillow. The snake tattoo wrapped around her neck to fall between her breasts to her navel.

How he longed to draw out the moment. To see her hips rise and fall to meet his strokes. To feel her wet warmth tighten around him. If he could memorize this very second, he would.

She reached up and stroked his face again. The ecstasy in her eyes made him smile.

"Zach, my love," she whispered.

Sliding into the warmth of her body, he groaned with contentment. At times like this, with her thighs clenching his hips and her breasts brushing against his chest, Zach fell into a place where all his worries disappeared and there was nothing left but Lark and him.

She moaned as he picked up the pace. Their pleasure was rising again. Much faster than he'd wanted. He clenched her tighter. She urged him to go faster. Soon enough, Lark stiffened underneath him, finding the peak he wanted her to reach.

All the while, he watched her, enjoying the arch of her back and her gasps of pleasure.

As he followed her soon after, he hoped this wouldn't be the last time they made love. That she would be open to him always.

FOR THE LONGEST OF TIME, THEY LAY WITH THEIR LIMBS intertwined. And Lark was perfectly happy with that. She sighed while he ran his fingers along her forehead.

"That feels nice," she purred.

He leaned in and kissed the spot.

Twice, she dozed off, only to wake up still in his arms. The sky outside had darkened, but the two of them were safe here—for now. She closed her eyes, and the only sound was the crashing of the waves against the pier outside.

"What are you thinking about?" he asked.

"The sea," she whispered. "It's an easy place to lose yourself."

"Yes, it can be."

A thought came to mind. She considered her words before she spoke them. "I can't stop thinking about the time when you left with Cyn. Back when she was really sick."

"Mm-hmm."

A pain circled her chest, but she forced herself to say the words. "Why didn't you tell me you were leaving? Did you ever think I wouldn't understand? That I wouldn't want the same thing for my dad?"

He froze beside her, then his hand drifted to caress her forehead again. "Yes, I've thought about it."

"I can't stop thinking about what I would've done if I had the opportunity to save my dad." Her throat dried. What she would've given for one more year with her dad. Hell, another day.

"You could've tried, but we both know Gio never would've let a werewolf heal him like Kaden did for Cyn."

"But what if I *forced* him to do it?" she asked, but she knew the answer, and it broke her heart. Her father never would've forgiven her.

But at least he'd be alive.

"You're right. A hunter like him would always be a hunter until the end." She sighed and snuggled against him.

The human heart was a complex thing.

"If a hunter never wavers from their cause, does that mean the Red clan will never stop hunting you?" she asked.

"Oh, they'll always want a piece of me." He gave her a kiss. Maybe to lighten her melancholy mood.

She rolled her eyes. "Oh, stop it. How about your hunters stand in line behind Justine? That would be nice."

The afternoon shadows in the room shifted as neither of them spoke.

"I wanted to leave yesterday," he said wistfully, "to protect you from them."

"And why didn't you?"

"I'm tired of running." He stroked the sensitive skin of her forearm, causing goosebumps to rise. "And I love you," he added softly.

Just hearing those words made her face fill with heat. Made her heart soar.

"So what do we do now?" she asked.

"I'm trying to think of anything I can do to keep the hunters away, but only an act of God will convince them otherwise."

An act of God.

An event resembling one could change everything.

She grinned at him. "I've got an idea, but you're not gonna like it. At all."

[25]

Zach absolutely hated the plan.

But as he hid and watched the ferry arrivals, he had to admit that Lark's idea could work if every step was executed perfectly.

"So why are we doing this again?" Brian asked from beside him.

"Because everyone has an agenda, and we can use that agenda against them." Just thinking about how it all tied to together left Zach in awe. "Have you ever wondered why the hunters or the werewolves didn't know about the witches?"

"Well, the witches sure as hell wouldn't put up a sign that they wanted to use us to protect their boxes."

Zach nodded. "And the human population, the hunters, didn't need to know about their existence or their cause. Lark told me that men reduce their strength. Their power lies in their privacy and seclusion."

Brian slowly nodded. "So that's why the hunters didn't believe me when I first told them you were hiding in a witches' camp." He sighed. "I ruined everything when I exposed the coven to the Red clan…and got you captured." Brian took in the town. "I'm still sorry about that."

Zach gripped his shoulder. He could understand why Brian did what he did, but they still had to clean up the mess from the aftermath.

He turned his attention to the incoming ferry. A large contingent of Red and Cerulean hunters arrived. His actions to draw the hunters to the mainland had only worked for so long. A few reconnaissance missions would've revealed that he never disembarked in Vancouver.

He swallowed a curse and pulled out his new burner phone. Six SUVs filled with hunters drove off the ferry and rolled into town. Even a military-grade Hummer rolled off the boat. He didn't want to know what equipment that held.

He sat still for so long that Brian asked, "You okay, man?"

"Yeah." Zach called a number he hadn't used in a long time. The caller didn't immediately pick up, but when he did, Zach almost hung up.

"Who is this?" Old Bart said gruffly.

"It's me."

His former teacher went quiet. "I didn't expect you to call this private line, Zachary."

Zach glanced at his watch. Bart would run a trace on him, but that didn't matter. "I didn't think you'd want to hear from me either, but I have something to tell you. A courtesy, if you will—"

"There is nothing to be said. You turned your back on your clan. On me, boy." Old Bart sounded tired.

"So the clan is all that matters? All the good things you taught me are still here. Respect. Kindness."

"And what of loyalty?"

"That's the reason I called." Time for Zach to end this and say his goodbyes. "There are things out there in the world the hunters haven't encountered yet. I have seen their power firsthand, Bart. Take your niece and leave the island."

His teacher went quiet again.

Zach gripped the phone tighter. "Tell the hunters to stay away—for your safety and their own."

"You know I can't do that… Good hunting to you, boy."

Then the line went dead.

Zach clenched the phone almost tight enough to break it, so he shoved it into his pocket. He'd done all he could do for his old family. Time to focus on the new one.

There would only be so much time before that caravan of hunters reached the training camp, then they'd spread all over the island to hunt him down. They would strike the witches too, with enough artillery to wipe them off the map.

TODAY WAS THE DAY.

Either Lark would be free from Justine or dead.

Maybe that was why it was so important for her to spend time with Iluminada. There was too much to do, and having Brian standing in her path to the main house didn't help.

"What do you want?" she said. Asking him again why he'd taken it upon himself to betray his friends—and she used that word loosely—was an exercise in futility.

Brian heaved out a sigh, and his exhale turned to frost. Yep, it was that damn cold outside, and she didn't feel like hanging out.

"I've tried to keep my distance." He finally forced himself to look her in the face. "You're mad, and you're right. I shouldn't have betrayed Zach or you." He shuffled a bit. "I want you to know I'm going to do everything within my power to show you can trust me. That Zach can trust me, too."

She searched his face, assessed his body language. Sincerity touched the wrinkles in his brow and regret pushed down his shoulders.

"And what will happen if you disagree with my actions in the future?" she asked.

He squeezed his eyes shut. "I will only act if your life is in *immediate* danger, but otherwise, I will listen for cues from…Zach."

"From Zach, huh?"

"Yeah, we came to an understanding, and I submitted to him as our alpha."

She didn't know if Brian had learned from what happened, but with time she might learn to trust him again.

"C'mon, then." She marched toward the main house again.

"Wh-where are we going?"

"I need to see my aunt before we head out. I don't know if…" She couldn't finish.

"When you fight Justine, you don't know what the outcome will be."

She nodded.

They approached the dark green house. Lark's pace was steady, but Brian's stride quickened.

Damn, she'd forgotten about the demon box.

She clutched Brian's arm. "You don't have to come with me. Return to the Lake House."

Brian blinked and backed up. "We need to find a way to secure that thing." He rubbed his forehead as if trying to shake off a headache. "If the demons are emitting a signal of some kind, with the right technology, we should be able to dampen it."

"That's a good idea." She patted his shoulder. "I hope to have the opportunity to come up with a solution."

Instead of finding her aunt in her room, Lark found

Iluminada waiting outside again. She sat on the main house swing. Lark joined her and set the bench in motion.

"How are you holding up, *mi hija*?" her aunt asked softly.

Lark weighed how to answer that question. She glanced at the forest beyond the courtyard, but the swaying pines held no answers.

"I'm fine…" she murmured. "No, I'm not fine. I'm still trying to sort through all of this and make it out to the other side."

Iluminada nodded. "Yeah, you've been through a lot."

"That is most certainly true." Lark sighed. "I'm not going to lie to you. This morning, I imagined I rented a boat and set sail across the Pacific."

Her aunt chuckled. "And where did you go?"

Lark told her about all the places she wished she could've seen. How she'd planned to travel more once she completed her graduate degree. All those plans to escape ended once Dad died.

"You can still go," Iluminada said. "Once everything quiets down again."

"I could go, but the question is: do I need to go anymore? Do I even need to finish my degree? I wanted to make things right after my dad died. And that meant repairing The Hunting Grounds, but now I realize I was trying to rebuild the wrong thing."

Iluminada grasped her hand and then released it. "You need to fix yourself first."

"Precisely."

She sighed. "But you must confront Justine first."

"That wasn't the self-growth I had planned."

"No, it wasn't, but I know you'll fight until the very end. With your family by your side, you can withstand anything."

Not far from them, the wind chimes on the back porch

clanged and tinkled. Iluminada drew a deep breath then retrieved something from her pocket and placed it in Lark's hand. "This is the only copy I have, but I want you to have it."

"Is this Mom?"

"That's my Lupita," Iluminada said softly.

Lark's mother, probably in her mid-teens, based on her womanly shape, stood next to the greenhouse. Her expression was pensive.

"She's so beautiful, yet sad."

"Lupita always had a faraway look in her eyes. You have the same thing."

Lark placed the photo in her pocket. If only she could float away like she did in her mind.

"You can withstand anything…" Someone else had told her those same words, but she rarely recalled that moment. Just thinking of the day she had to drive her dad to the hospice center threatened to steal her breath away. At the time, she'd believed the world would end.

NINE MONTHS AGO

"HEY, SWEETIE, YOU GONNA PUT DOWN THAT SPONGE?" Dad asked Lark from the other side of the kitchen. "It's time to go."

Lark had heard Dad ask her if she was ready ten minutes ago, but she'd found something else in the kitchen to clean. She surveyed the room. Everything was in its place. The fridge, stove, and counters still gleamed. The family photo— with Mom and Dad holding a squirmy five-year-old Lark— was positioned perfectly in the center of the fridge. Every corner and hiding spot for dirt, grime, and dust had been uncovered.

There was nothing left to do but drive Dad to Pearlman's Hospice Center.

The keys sat in her back pocket, but the need to find something—anything—else to do flicked at her.

"Pop, you need help to get in the car?" she asked him.

Her dad grunted, his standard reply whenever she offered assistance and didn't want any.

Giovanni DeStefano still towered over her, but his once-wide barrel chest had narrowed. The strong arms that had held her as a child now barely got him through daily tasks like dressing and showering.

Dad stared at her and ran his hands over the black and white stubble on his chin. The hair had begun to grow back after he'd ended his chemotherapy a while ago.

No more treatments. The thought stabbed her soul, and almost stole her breath.

She took a deep breath, adding strength to her weakening resolve. She grabbed her dad's coat and helped him into it.

Right outside the window, thick snow covered the houses in the quiet South Vancouver neighborhood. When her dad didn't accept the gloves or scarf, she gave him the *look*.

He pursed his lips and let her slide the gloves over his trembling hands. Had his pain medication worn off already? His uncontrolled pain and nausea remained a persistent problem. She wrapped the scarf around his neck, trying not to take in his face or the stoic expression he always had.

I can't break. Not right now, she thought.

Fifteen years ago, it was her dad who'd stood in this very spot and bundled her up to play down the street at MacDonald Park. Back then, she'd always been in a hurry—far more eager than her dad to run around with the neigh-borhood kids.

How she wished she hadn't been in such a hurry back then. Maybe she could've stretched out the time with him.

With Dad wrapped in multiple layers, she followed him out the front door to the car. She'd warmed the vehicle up already—only to go back into the house. Now they plodded down the cleared sidewalk to Dad's trusty Volvo V6. Soon enough, they were inside and off to their next destination.

While she drove with the heat on full blast, she waited for him to speak. Usually, he talked her head off about the Canucks and how great, or badly, they'd played their last game.

"Hey, Pop, you want Aunt Gretchen to make you some taco soup—" she began.

"It's okay, Lark."

Her forehead furrowed.

"I know what you're thinking, but baby it's okay." He chuckled a bit then winced. "I might be heading to the center, but this isn't the end. The docs said anything is possible."

Yes, anything was possible, but she'd sat in the same room and heard the dire news, too. She wanted to make sure he was comfortable.

Dad continued. "You remind me a lot of your mom. She always had a lot on her mind, but I believed she could withstand anything."

He patted her shoulder. "We all share the same fears, but it's our determination, that hunger to take another blow and be ready to stand up again, that will help us weather this moment."

Dad settled into the seat and closed his eyes, but the warmth from his reassuring touch and his words remained.

She prayed they always would.

[26]

ONCE THE TEMPERATURE ROSE FIFTEEN DEGREES OVER an hour and the sea level lifted above the piers, the witches prepared for Justine's arrival.

The first order of business was Katia. When Lark and Yolande entered the witch's cell, she stared at them blankly until Yolande snapped, "Get up. You're coming with us."

No one said a word as Lark drove the two of them to Snug Cove to drop off Katia.

After Yolande deposited the wide-eyed and untied witch by the side of the road, Lark said, "Tell your employer I'll meet her tonight in the Fairy Fen Nature Preserve…if she dares."

On the way back to the coven, it was all seriousness until Yolande started laughing.

"What?" Lark asked.

Yolande mocked her with a serious face. "Tell that bitch to come get me…if she dares…" She laughed again, and Lark flipped her off.

"What else am I supposed to say—I didn't say *bitch*, but I should have?"

237

Seeing Yolande smile was refreshing, even if she was making fun of her. "No, no, you did fine. You were a badass, actually."

"Good."

They pulled up to the courtyard and parked. Once they left the car, the camaraderie ended.

It was time for the witches to gather.

They entered the main house and headed to the great room. Lark had never seen everyone gather at once. The witchlings sat on the floor while the adults waited for them on chairs.

Zenobia stood before everyone and gestured for Lark and Yolande to join them. "We're all here now. Good."

She turned to the younger witches, and their quiet chatter ended. "When I was young, I never knew danger. The elders in my coven never told me when a demon arrived or left, or a box was compromised." She sighed. "That ignorance allowed me to be a child, but I was never ready to face my adversaries. I won't do such a thing to you."

Her stern eye swept over the witchlings until she had their attention. "One of our sisters is coming. She means one of us harm, so we must *defend* the Painted Coven. You will do your part by listening to your older sisters. No fighting. No misbehaving. Understood?"

The witchlings' heads bobbed.

Zenobia focused on the other witches in the room with a harsher tone. "As we have planned, the young witches will remain with the caregivers in the Gossamer House cellar. Yolande and Jamilah, it will be your responsibility to ensure their safety."

The blood witch enforcers inclined their heads.

"My sisters," Zenobia said, "a great storm is coming today. The likes of which you'll never see again in your life-time. Some of the elders may not return today, but you must not mourn us. You must continue our ways. Teach the blood craft. Be prepared for the day when you too will be called to defend us."

Lark took in the whole room. None of their faces showed fear. Only perseverance.

Once the children and the rest of the sisters left the room, Fredda stood. Lark and Zenobia followed her to the coat rack.

"At least it's warmer outside," Fredda mused aloud.

"I don't know about warm," Lark said, "but it's not below *freezing* anymore."

That got a soft laugh from Zenobia, who, Lark noted, appeared frailer today. If not, perhaps just tired. "We'll be warm soon enough," the elder witch added.

Fredda helped Zenobia slip into her black coat while Lark did the same for Fredda.

Lark put on hers last.

After Lark was dressed, Zenobia clasped Fredda's hand and squeezed it. Fredda took Lark's hand. Lark completed the circle by taking Zenobia's right.

Then the women exchanged a long look as Lark's serpent slid across her back to settle over her fast-beating heart.

"Time for us to end this," Fredda murmured.

"Are you ready?" Zenobia asked Lark.

"Yes." There was one more crucial step to take, but she was *finally* ready.

THERE WAS NO DOUBT IN ZACH'S MIND NOW: *JUSTINE IS coming.*

To the northwest, the sky darkened further. More warm rain fell and left the forest muddy and full of shadows. It was still a perfect hunting ground for wolves.

From his spot along the tree line in the courtyard, Zach tilted his snout to the heavens. Not far from him, Janet and Brian paced the courtyard. Their scents exuded restlessness. Uncertainty. Perhaps they too sensed the oncoming disaster.

The blackness in the sky drew closer. It spread like an advancing leviathan, its tentacles eating away at the light. From within its depths, flashes of lightning streaked across the menacing clouds. Many spears of light raced to the ground and struck the island. The ground beneath his feet shuddered. The wolves around him whined.

He rose and circled them to offer reassurance. Across the courtyard, the back door to the main house opened. Lark emerged. Fredda and Zenobia followed her.

As the women strode toward the sedan, he hurried over to join them. The older witch paid him no mind and got into the passenger seat. The witch Lark had called Fredda slipped into the driver seat.

Lark paused next to the sedan. She took in the growing gloom with an expression he couldn't read. He brushed his flank against her legs. When she didn't respond, he licked her fingers.

That made her smile briefly before her brow furrowed and her lips formed a thin line. She had minimal fear, but he couldn't place where her thoughts lay.

She picked up the supplies pack next to the car and opened the trunk to place the backpack inside. Then she opened the passenger door and looked his way.

There's no turning back now.

Before he leapt inside, he gave a look to Brian and Janet. *It's time.*

With a yip, they disappeared into the woods. Brian knew where they needed to go.

Zach jumped into the back seat, and Lark followed.

There was little room left for her, but she snuggled against him nonetheless.

No one spoke during the drive toward the preserve. Maybe they considered what needed to be done, like he had. Again and again, he'd tried to drill as many holes through Lark's idea as he could—but it was sound.

As long as Justine's actions could be predicted.

Beside him, Lark rested her head against his neck. She stroked his fur, the other hand clenched into a fist.

Was she in pain?

Briefly, he turned toward her, but she wouldn't face him. She simply stared out the window as they drove downhill away from Mt. Gardner. The reserve lay several miles to the south.

By the time they'd entered the park's outskirts, rain soaked the streets. The wind shook the trees.

Zenobia placed her coat's hood over her head, and Fredda did the same.

Zach scanned the outside for danger. The reserve parking lot was nearly empty. Few people would be out at this time of the year exploring the wetlands. They were at least half a mile from the training camp.

Zenobia parked the car, and the witches got out. Lark retrieved the pack from the trunk. She left it right next to the car. If the wolves shifted back to their human form, the clothes would prove useful. From the pack, Lark retrieved and loaded a Kimber Warrior pistol. She slipped the weapon into her coat's inner pocket.

He definitely approved of that choice.

When all plans fail, open fire and shoot.

The storm was almost over them now. Little remained of the November sky as shadows swept over the forest. Soon day would become night.

I must defend them until the end, he reminded himself.

He led the women into the woods. If they encountered any Red clan tripwires or traps, he wanted to divert their path.

Minutes later, he spied the camp outskirts. All the lights above the trailers cast a glow along the thrashing trees. The wind's roar increased.

To his dismay, all the vehicles remained. Every window in the trailers were lit and shadows shifted as hunters moved about.

They hadn't heeded his warnings.

He turned to Lark. She held up the rear with ashen features. Was she well enough to complete the plan?

"She's almost here," Zenobia said with a growing smile. "Soon, we'll play again, my witchling."

When the storm's violent winds rattled the trailers, it didn't take long for the base to flare to life.

Hunters rushed from buildings like scattering ants. If Zach had planned it right, they'd go to the storm shelter.

Only a handful raced for the refuge.

Shit.

The witches huddled near the trees to avoid debris. They'd have to find a safe place soon too—and that meant either hiding or confronting Justine sooner than they'd planned.

They didn't have to wait long.

The dark clouds above churned and slowly began to circle.

On the other side of the camp, Zach watched a lone middle-aged woman wearing a long white coat emerge from between cedar trees. Determination lined her angular, yet soft features. She strode toward the camp, and the stench of blood followed. Now that she was closer, he could make out her pointed chin, elfin-like, tiny nose, and high cheekbones. Wisps of curly black hair clung to her forehead.

What couldn't be missed: the trail of blood streaking down her pearl coat from a cut on her neck to the ground. And the crimson-stained knife in her right hand.

The hunters were on her in an instant.

Over the screaming wind, he strained to hear them call out to her.

"Do you need help?" one of them yelled. "You should come inside!"

Run. They ignored Zach's pleas. *Aren't the evacuation orders in effect?*

Justine replied to one hunter, but Zach couldn't make out what she said.

Only that her reply wasn't what they wanted to hear—the closest hunter pointed a handgun in her direction.

The witch flashed a Cheshire-like smile before she extended a bloody left hand in the air. More hunters took aim.

Oh, no.

Lightning danced across the heavens. Static electricity built. The need to rush to his former team fought with the need to keep the witches safe.

Suddenly, a white-hot lightning bolt shot down, connected with the middle of Justine's bloodstained palm, and snaked out to impale the hunters around her.

Zach watched with horror as their sizzling bodies crashed to the wet ground.

"She is the devil himself under the guise of an angel," Yolande had said.

Justine stepped around the men to head deeper into the training camp. The hunters who opened fire in her direction got the same treatment.

As the whole landscape around them filled with lightning strikes and the stench of ozone, Zenobia made her move, and the other witches followed.

Janet and Brian raced in from the north to join them.

Good. They were all together now.

Zenobia edged along the southern edge of the camp past the first trailer. Everyone formed a line behind her. At least one hundred yards away, Justine approached the first trailer on the northeastern side of the camp.

A hunter fleeing Justine appeared. It was a student. The frightened young man stared wide-eyed at the elder witch.

"Do you wish to die too?" she barked.

The boy shuffled then stumbled to escape into the woods.

Without another word, Zenobia motioned for them to keep moving. They finally reached the open door of a trailer. She gestured for Fredda to act.

Fredda's figure wavered then went out of focus to a blur. She stepped into the trailer.

Then the screams began.

Four men in fatigues escaped from the trailer into the night. What had she done to them?

Once the trailer was empty, everyone hurried inside as Justine checked the second trailer.

Zenobia reached for Lark's right hand and grasped it. "We don't have much time. Everyone else, let's go." She paused to catch her breath. "Lark, stay inside as long as you can. She'll strike you down from a distance. We must do everything we can to get you as close to her as possible."

"Why can't we wait for her outside?" Lark asked. "Couldn't she could pick up this trailer *Wizard of Oz*-style?"

Fredda chuckled. "Crushing you under a house is way too easy. Justine can't gloat and savor the moment if she can't do the *deed* in person."

The lights above them flickered then went out. Brian whined while Janet circled Lark's legs.

Outside the window, they observed Justine. She was heading in their direction—until the opening of the storm shelter caught her eye.

"She's not coming anymore," Zenobia said.

Zach growled.

Those hunters would have nowhere to go.

He glanced at the other wolves, and the guardians raced out of the trailer.

"We'll get her back on track," Fredda said firmly. "And when the opportunity arises, I will *kill* her. This is ridiculous."

"No." Lark grabbed her arm. "Remember the plan."

"Did you see what she did to those people?" Fredda said. "We've known her longer than you have. She doesn't care. Neither should you."

Lark blinked slowly. "Yes, I should care. We are *not* going to kill her. We all have a purpose, and she has hers. Buy me time to get close to her."

Zenobia followed Fredda out.

Zach ran for the door to follow the others but glanced over his shoulder.

Lark stood there. One of her hands trembled and she clenched her teeth. Was leaving a wise choice? He'd left her behind too many times in the past. He almost considered staying when Lark spoke.

"I'll be fine. Go!" she said vehemently. "Save them and *bring* her to me. I got this."

$$[\ 27\ ]$$

Lark peered out the windows to see the werewolves circling Justine in a pincer movement. Zenobia and Fredda advanced in unison, approaching her head-on. A true fight.

But what were the witches doing? Wouldn't Justine have to go through them to reach Lark?

Fear rocketed through her, and her desire to follow the plan faltered. She clutched at the object in her inner pocket.

They're all going to die, the serpent said, cackling. *Their blood will cover the ground and feed me well. Feed us.*

No.

Focus, she reminded herself.

When her heartbeat steadied again, she returned to the window. Before Justine reached the storm cellar, the wolves attacked her. Zach leapt onto the storm cellar doors, snapping and growling at her. His hazel eyes flashed with fury.

But Justine was ready for them. Her left hand shot in the air. Small lightning bolts struck the ground near their feet, but the nimble wolves kept advancing and retreating faster than she could strike.

The pack forced her toward the witches.

And at least one of the witches had to be in striking distance now.

"Come for me, you miserable bitch!" Fredda called out.

Justine shuddered then glanced wide-eyed at her blood-stained hand as if she saw something ominous. With a choked cry, Justine scratched at her wrist. Swiped at her arms.

All the while, the wolves skulked toward her from behind, edging forward with their teeth bared. Zenobia inched her way past Fredda toward Justine.

Lark crept toward the door. The time to act was coming. If only Zenobia could briefly blind Justine for Lark to approach her.

Briefly, Justine's gaze connected with Fredda.

"Your parlor tricks don't scare me *anymore*." With deft precision, Justine cut deep along her chin, drew a glyph on her palm, then flexed her left fist.

Zenobia extended her hand toward Justine. The elder witch's eyes turned black.

Time paused—or it seemed to for Lark as she held her breath.

Suddenly, everything went white. Hundreds of lightning bolts punched the earth, forcing Lark to shut her eyes. A blindingly white light snaked through the room and struck the middle. Searing heat filled the trailer. A thunderous clap smacked Lark's ears before she was swept off her feet and propelled into the nearest wall.

She landed hard on the linoleum floor.

Don't let it go, she thought. *I must hold myself together.*

The snake slithered back and forth along her spine. It slurped the suffering around her and fed freely.

She wrenched herself up. Smoke from a growing fire on the other end of the trailer pushed her back to the exit.

Please be alive, Zach, she prayed.

Lark stumbled out of the trailer to a scorched landscape. Tiny fires flickered from struck brush in the forest. Mangled and burned vehicles drenched the camp with the stench of acrid chemicals.

And bodies lay everywhere.

No, Zach, no.

She searched for him and spotted the witches first. Fredda lay unconscious on her side, while not far from her, Zenobia's curled-up form rested against a turned-over trailer.

Behind Justine, her other victims—three dark wolves—were sprawled around the storm shelter doors.

Lark waited two breaths for Zach's chest to move. A brief shudder. Nothing more.

Instead of allowing the shock to bury her, she channeled the feeling where it needed to go. Into what she had no choice but to do.

She was truly the last one standing.

The rain ceased and the wind settled.

"You were wise to wait for me," Justine whispered with a small smile. Less blood dripped from the cut on her cheek, but Lark didn't doubt the witch had power left.

Focus, Lark reminded herself. Her burden to hold would be lifted soon.

She approached Justine.

Hold on, Zach. Just a little bit longer. Your actions won't be in vain.

Justine's grin widened. "Folake always ran away from me, but you beckoned me with open arms. I rather enjoyed that."

Lark unzipped her coat and palmed the weapon. The Kimber Warrior reassured her, but that wasn't what she needed to retrieve.

"Are you going to shoot me?" Justine said as if she didn't care.

"No," Lark said. "This was for the hunters. While this"—she retrieved a scarf-covered package from deep within her pocket—"is what I brought for you."

Without flourish, Lark removed the red silk scarf to reveal the beautiful cigar box.

You are free to sing now, my pretties.

She *released* her hold over them with a long exhale.

For the past half hour, Lark had done as Fredda had taught. She'd used her personal pain and sorrow, Dad's death up to the events of the last couple of days, to feed the serpent and have it do *her* bidding. Every tear she'd shed had prepared her for today.

The witch's mouth dropped and her face went ashen. "No…"

She shuffled backward.

The demons trapped inside the box had to be a choir singing the most hypnotic hymn.

"You wanted the serpent, Justine," Lark spat. "Strike me down like you've always wanted."

Justine trembled, her whole body shaking as she fought the demon's cry for her to touch the box's surface.

"I can end your suffering and silence the box again." Lark extended the container. The wood hummed and vibrated against her fingers.

"Give her the box," the serpent intoned. *"Let her taste us."*

"Clever witch." Justine strained to back away.

"But you don't want that, do you?" Lark crept forward. "Come kill me then."

Justine clawed at the dirt to crawl away from Lark. "I could kill the world if that thing possesses me—"

"Yes, you could, but innately, you *want* to protect. Not harm. You might want to strike me down, but I don't want to end your life—or destroy the world. If my demon was truly in control of my actions, weaponizing you would be the ulti-mate kill shot."

"Bring them to her," the serpent begged. *"Look what she did to your mate. Let them tear her soul apart."*

The strain on Justine's face amplified. Lark could imagine the destruction if the demons possessed the powerful blood witch. Bowen Island would be first, then the mainland would follow. One dead body after another. Including Zach's. All those deaths could be prevented. Even if Lark wanted Justine to suffer for what she did.

Mercy begins today. I've tortured her enough.

Lark retreated, and Justine shuddered.

"Return to the mainland," Lark commanded her. "No more attacks. Tell the other witches to stay away too."

"But what if—"

"What if the serpent tries to influence me?" Lark shook her head. "When Folake gave me this thing, she told me I was a part of the circle now. A path I could never escape." She snorted. "Fuck that shit."

Justine scrambled to stand. The heated glare she threw at Lark could've boiled her alive.

"I'm not Folake," Lark said. "Nor will I ever be."

Lark silenced the demons again. Once free from the call, Justine crawled to the nearest trailer to add distance between them.

"You can't hold them forever," she whispered, the strength in her words gone. "The demon inside you will fight until it controls everything."

"It serves a purpose. Just like you served a purpose against the hunters," Lark said. "Goodbye, dear sister. I hope I won't have to bring *our* friends to your doorstep."

Lark walked toward the witch again until Justine scram-bled to run away from the camp. With her enemy on the run, Lark hurried to check on Fredda. She was unconscious, but her chest rose and fell with shallow breaths. Zenobia didn't fare well, but hearing a moan when Lark touched her face briefly gave her relief.

Dread returned as Lark approached the wolves. First, she checked Janet. Her back was broken, but she'd live. Not far from Janet, another black wolf fought for each wet breath. Lark ran her hand along Brian's flank, and his pained whimper sliced through her. How many internal injuries did he have?

God help me, please let Zach not be this way.

She didn't want to see the final wolf who lay a few feet away. She didn't want to see or know. Her chin trembled and her insides began to quake.

He couldn't be dead.

But the wolf's chest didn't rise and fall.

Zachary…

With a sorrowful moan, she slipped out of her coat and placed it over him. Then she lay down next to him on the cold, wet ground and wrapped her arms around Zach's neck.

She ran her fingers through his fur, fighting against the need to bury her face against him and scream. Love had brought them this far, hadn't it?

Suddenly, fur became warm skin. The black wolf's elongated snout collapsed to become a man's face. And finally, Zach's eyes popped open.

Lark's mouth opened wide as Zach slipped his arms around her waist and drew her close. She placed her hand on his chest and felt his heartbeat.

He was alive. How?

"I thought you were dead," she whispered.

That familiar smirk lit up his face. "Just needed a little shuteye to heal. Believe me, I'm hurt pretty badly, but I told you, baby. I'm not leaving you anymore. Not for death. Not for anything." Zach kissed the top of her head, then pressed his nose there and inhaled.

With a laugh, she replied, "That you did."

Time flitted along. Maybe it was a few precious seconds. Maybe it was nothing more than a couple of minutes. When Zach stood again and donned her long coat, she reluctantly let him go.

She watched him attend to one witch after another to heal them. From one wolf to the injured hunter lying next to them. They all received his care.

Lark turned to face the sky as twilight began to fall. Snowflakes swayed with the breeze.

They'd survived this fight. And they'd survived the next one together. Both the hunter *and* werewolf had returned to her. Safe and sound.

Lark smiled as she returned to Bowen Island again. The ferry pulled up to the Snug Cove dock, and the touchdown buoyed Lark's spirits.

I'm home again, she thought.

She glanced at Zach in the driver's seat. He patted her thigh in response. Did he feel at ease again now that they were home?

After spending a long morning into the afternoon in Vancouver, it lightened her mood to see less cityscape, more rustic buildings, trees, and wildlife.

But the trip had been necessary. After living for a month on Bowen Island and experiencing the events from Justine's attack to the arrival of the demon box and learning of her true heritage, Lark was ready to make painful decisions.

"You want to stop for anything at the Snug Cove store?" he asked.

"We've got enough supplies," she said.

"We do," added Janet from the back seat.

"But what if they finally have some Almond Joy?" Zach asked with a mischievous smile.

Good God. How long had it been since Lark had had one? The last time had been when she'd dropped off Zach before she crossed the border back into Canada.

She'd put up every wall she could think of to forget about him, but her heart thought otherwise.

"We can go back after Christmas," she said. "It's been a long day, and I can wait."

Yes, it had been a long day.

Six hours ago, she'd finalized the sale for The Hunting Grounds. The place was her last connection with her dad, but the profits and his memory would carry her for the years to come.

Zach reached over and took her hand. Strength lay in his reassuring grip. Even the ever-present serpent quieted on her torso.

After the signing, all she'd needed to do was pack up what few belongings she had in her apartment in Seattle and say goodbye to family. Telling Dad's family about Zach and her guardians was never a part of the plan, but at least divulging that she'd found a final home and was safe gave them relief.

Their niece wouldn't be jumping from one job to another anymore.

As they pulled in to the courtyard, she spied several witchlings gathering on the Gossamer House back porch. Did they have an idea what she had?

The elder witches assembled to greet them too. Fredda, Zenobia, and Iluminada gathered on the main house porch.

Of course, the trailer hitched to their new SUV had caught everyone's attention. Lark, Brian, and Janet got out to help unload things, but Zach waited inside to stare at the Christmas decorations lighting up the forest around the courtyard.

~

DAMN, ZACH LOVED CHRISTMASTIME. WATCHING THE flashing white, green, and red lights among the pine trees quieted the wolf stirring within him.

Was his sister enjoying the holidays with Kaden in Montana? He hoped. He had memories of snowball fights with Ty and creeping around with Cyn to shake the Christmas presents. He wouldn't be spending the holidays with her—and most certainly not with his hunter brother Ty —but he had a new family.

A new pack to take care of for the days to come.

"Home isn't the house you live within," his sister had told him. *"It's the people inside of it."*

Cyn was right.

He got out of the car to offer a hand. He smiled to see the witchlings had been busy while they'd been gone all day. The holiday decorations that he'd bought with Brian last week had gone to good use.

He'd learned the coven had never celebrated Christmas. Matter of fact, the strange look Yolande had given him after he bought the two boxes still made him chuckle.

"What a waste of time," she'd said. "And money. Witchlings should be studying."

Her daughter Sylvia's squeal of delight told him that the little girl didn't agree with her mother.

Before they'd set out for Vancouver, Zach and Brian had hung up wreaths and lights on the Lake House. The second box had mysteriously disappeared, and now its contents hung on the Gossamer House.

Bah humbug avoided, he thought with a nod.

But there was more work to be done.

He joined Lark and the others unloading the trailer.

"Are you sure these supplies will work?" she asked him.

Over the last couple of weeks, he'd had a lot of time to work with Brian on securing the demon box. As a risk-assessment analyst, Brian had picked apart Zach's ideas, but together they'd developed a magic- and technology-based solution.

"It should work," he replied. "How come no one ever created a warded room with access panels?"

She shrugged. "Maybe the witches have been set in their ways for too long. Either way, by the time we finish everything, we won't have to worry about the witches or the wolves stumbling into the room."

Her face hardened with determination. "By the time we're done with this place, I want Bowen Island to be a prison for every single demon box out there."

"And it will be a safe haven for everyone." He drew her to his side. She snuggled against him.

He surveyed the forest beyond the courtyard. The flashing lights hid the forest beyond, but soon the coven's camp would expand. More cottages. And more fortifications to keep the children safe. Soon the pack would be prepared for anything or anyone who'd dare return.

And if they had to fight again, they'd face those dangers together.

The End

COVETED

"A regular person in a magical body, Natalya's struggles with her job (irritable Harpies trying to return vases!) and love life are both hilarious and heartwarming."

—NYT Bestselling Author Eloisa James
Reading Romance Column
B&N Review

Prequel
Novella
0.5

Book
1

Book
2

Novella
2.5

Book
3

Short Story
Collection

Prequel feat.
Aggie
McClure

VALKYRIE
RISING
PRESS

ABOUT THE AUTHOR

Shawntelle Madison is a Web developer who loves to weave words as well as code. She'd be reluctant to admit it, but if pressed, she'd say that she covets and collects source code. After losing her first summer job detasseling corn, Madison performed various jobs, from fast-food clerk to grunt programmer to university webmaster. Writing eccentric characters is her favorite job of all. On any given day when she's not surgically attached to her computer, she can be found watching cheesy horror movies or the latest action-packed anime. Shawntelle Madison lives in Missouri with her husband and children.